"I KNOW NO LADY WOULD COME UP HERE LIKE THIS,"

Willena said quietly, a tremor in her voice.

"She might," Longarm whispered, "if she really wanted to."

She sank down beside him and exhaled heavily. "I really wanted to," she said. "I lay in my bed down there, but all I could think of was you up here."

He drew her down beside him and kissed her lips gently. He loosened the single button that fastened her blue denim shirt. It fell open and he felt her body quiver in reaction. He closed his hand over the high-standing globe of her breast. He heard her gasp for breath.

"Oh, yes," she whispered. "Oh, I needed your hands on me like that...."

TABOR EVANS

IN THE BIG THICKET

A JOVE BOOK

LONGARM IN THE BIG THICKET

A Jove Book / published by arrangement with
the author

PRINTING HISTORY
Jove edition / October 1982

ISBN: 0-515-05604-9

PRINTED IN THE UNITED STATES OF AMERICA

Chapter 1

Longarm awoke suddenly to the pounding of heavy, impatient fists rattling the door panel.

"All right," he said. "All right."

The harsh brilliance of the high-country morning sunlight poured through the open, curtained window and reflected on the badly polished oakwood flooring. Longarm swung his long legs over the side of the bed and poised there for a moment, trying to get his bearings. Then his gaze touched on the man sprawled on the other bed, still asleep—Deputy U. S. Marshal Wally Cochrane, his partner on this investigation.

He hadn't wanted Chi Cochrane. It wasn't really personal; Longarm never wanted any partner. He worked better alone. But he'd been stunned into assenting silence when Chief Marshal Billy Vail told him, "Chi Cochrane is assigned to this case. It's his. He's been working on it for months. You're siding him, Long."

Staring at Cochrane's sleeping face, Long remembered sharply the sinking sense of shock, almost as if he were being handed a demotion for good work, at being sent on a case as an assistant. It hadn't made sense then and it didn't make sense

1

now. That wasn't the way he worked. That wasn't the way Billy Vail used him.

Cochrane's fat, florid face was warped in his sleep by a wide grin. Looking down at the sleeping deputy, Longarm shook his head. He sure as hell didn't know what Chi had to grin about. The case was going badly; going nowhere, in fact. They'd followed a lot of blind trails flush into blank walls. And in the middle of the night, Cochrane hadn't looked this pleased. Longarm had awakened to find him standing in his union suit at the open window. Shoulders round, Cochrane had stood slumped, staring down at Golden's main street.

Longarm exhaled, taking his Colt .44-40 from under his pillow as the fists resumed punishing the door frame. Something had been troubling Cochrane last night, but you'd never guess it now, seeing that flushed, full-cheeked face grinning in undisturbed sleep while the hotel rattled around him.

Shaking his head, Longarm padded barefoot across the room. In his skin-tight longjohns, he was a lean, muscular man with shoulders that flared out straight and squared. His raw-boned face was wind-cured, his skin browned the color of saddle leather by hot suns on remote trails. There was no suggestion of softness about him, not even in the gunmetal blue of his habitually squinted, watchful eyes. His close-cropped hair was the burnt shade of old tobacco leaves, as was the longhorn mustache waxed neatly across his upper lip.

As those fists started a renewed tattoo on the door, Longarm growled through it, "Keep your goddamn shirt on."

"Open up in there." The voice was loud, sharp, and forceful.

Longarm held his Colt casually at his side and took his time unlocking the door. He kept his foot against the bottom frame of the door and opened it, holding it only slightly ajar.

Eyes widening, Longarm recognized Sheriff Lyle Dexter and two of his deputies. Angus Craft and Ernie Gage backed their boss, guns drawn, faces cold. And Dexter held a double-barreled shotgun in his fist like a handgun.

Longarm felt as if the world had waked up crazy this morning. His association with Dexter's office had been cordial, if less than warm. He and Cochrane had worked as well with the sheriff these past days as Federal marshals usually worked with local lawmen. But there was no trace of cordiality in Dexter's hard-eyed face this morning.

Longarm peered at them through the crack in the doorway.

"What's going on? You fellows trying to tear down the door?"

"If we have to." Sheriff Dexter's voice shook with suppressed rage. He was a rotund, graying county official with a trained politician's counterfeit features, made to smile and dissemble, but a range rider's rough voice and forthright manner. Right now, Dexter looked more than ready to use the shotgun quivering in his callused fist. "Why don't you let us ask the questions, Long?" he went on.

Longarm managed to bite back the sudden gorge of outrage. He kept his voice flat, moving his chilly gaze from the sheriff to his heavy-set deputies, gone fat at the public trough. Not one of them would he hire to enforce animal ordinances. Craft was cunning; that was apparent in his face. Gage was stupid; that was obvious too. But Gage was something more. He was a fast gun, an hombre who read *Ned Buntline's True Tales of the Wild West* and accepted every word as gospel.

Longarm shook his head. "What the hell is this, Dexter?"

"I told you, Long, we'll ask any goddamn questions." Dexter's rough voice reverberated along the silent second-floor hallway.

Longarm tried to smile, but failed. "You better go have another cup of coffee and try again, Sheriff."

"Don't tell me what to do."

"You and me are sure as hell going to tangle, Lyle, if you keep yelping like that," Longarm said.

"You son of a bitch," Dexter said. "Don't threaten me."

Longarm forced himself to laugh. "Under the circumstances, Sheriff, I figured I was being friendly."

Dexter stared at Longarm for a long beat, rage seething in his unflinching gray eyes. Then, his mouth twisting in contempt, the sheriff turned his head and jerked it toward his deputies in some sort of signal.

Watching the sheriff in stunned amazement, Longarm was caught off-guard by the big man's sudden movement. As Dexter turned back to face Longarm, he lunged abruptly forward from the balls of his big feet, driving his beefy shoulder against the door. He could have moved boulders with less force. The door went flying open. It jammed Longarm's toes back toward his heels and he yelped, leaping aside and jerking up his gun. He stared into the double barrels on the shotgun as the three men strode into the room.

Longarm shrugged. "I think you're crazy, Dexter, going

3

against a Federal badge. But, for the moment, it looks like you hold the aces. You want to tell me now what the hell you're after?"

"You crooked son of a bitch." Dexter thrust the gun barrel forward and Longarm retreated a step, lowering his Colt to his side. His rage was huge enough to include his partner, who snored through all this, sleeping when he needed him. "We got you cold, Long." Dexter's voice shook in self-righteous fury. "You made a mess this time, and you'd best stand easy and let me handle it. My boys would as soon put bullets in your rotten gut as look at you."

"Yeah," Ernie Gage said. He twisted his head like a vulture scanning its prey.

"I don't suppose you want to tell me what you're talking about?" Longarm inquired.

"No, damn it, I don't mind running through it. But you know it a hell of a lot better than we do. But not better than we will before we're through with you over at the county jail," Dexter said.

"Yeah." Gage craned his neck again, his strange eyes glittering.

"Lowest son of a bitch in my book," Dexter said, "is a lawman who betrays his oath, uses his goddamn shield as armor to pull off his dirty work."

"And that's got you in an uproar—about me?"

Dexter stared at Longarm murderously for ten full, slow seconds. Twice he seemed about to speak, but changed his mind. Instead of answering Longarm, but without taking his alert gaze from the deputy's face, the sheriff spoke over his shoulder. "Angus. Check the bastard's boots."

His rage rising, Longarm said, "You better make your charges, Dexter, before your boys get you in water that's gonna scald your ass up to your eyebrows."

"Shut up, killer," the sheriff said as if barely able to speak to him. "If you had one lick of sense, you'd keep your mouth shut." The sheriff spoke now with a terrible, forced patience that seemed to vibrate under the pressures roiling inside him. "We got you cold. And we got witnesses here, and every damn word you say is going to be used against you."

Longarm shrugged his tight longjohns up on his shoulders. "I'm warning you, Dexter. For the last time. Make your charges."

"This is my county, Long. These are my deputies. Nobody's going to be listening to you, unless you're ready to confess to robbery and murder."

"Robbery and murder, eh? Is that just for starters? Show me a warrant or get your fat killers out of here."

Dexter opened his mouth to rage back at Longarm, but hesitated and spoke with the sort of calm reserved to those who are certain they're right. "All right. I'm charging you with aidin' an' abettin' road agents and murderers. Is that good enough? And even more than that, if the evidence I'm looking for against you proves out, I'm charging you with grand larceny and murder."

Longarm drew a deep breath. He felt the tightening of nerves in the pit of his belly. There was no doubting the big sheriff's sincerity of his total belief in his position. "Mind saying what I stole—and who I killed?"

For a long beat those savage gray eyes struck against Longarm's raging gunmetal blue ones. "Pete Hayes," Dexter said at last, "driver for the Freedom Mine, killed. Kaliope Zembillas, the shotgun, lies wounded and unconscious. Crimes committed in the robbery of a Freedom Mine stage loaded with processed gold ore from the smelter. Is that good enough for a start?"

"You're out of your head. You know damned good and well it's that kind of gang we're up here investigating," Longarm said.

"Makes it convenient for you, don't it, killer?"

Before Longarm could speak, Angus Craft returned from the side of Longarm's mussed bed, carrying his left boot.

A glitter of triumph fired the sheriff's fat-socketed gray eyes. He said, "These your boots, Long?" It was a statement rather than a question. His voice quavered with victory. "You're damn right they're your boots. Fancy cavalry style. Knowed you for a dude the minute I spied them fancy boots. Never saw no other lawman, or anybody else outside the cavalry, with boots like 'em."

Longarm shrugged. "They're easy to walk in. I do more walking than riding."

He exhaled heavily. They were not listening. They were checking his boots. The heel was gone from the left one. He knew damned well he'd walked into this room last night, sober, under his own power, wearing his own boots, with both heels.

5

He hadn't limped in here—he'd walked in.

Without bothering to glance at Longarm, the sheriff took a small black boot heel from his jacket pocket. With much ceremony, he pressed it in place upon Longarm's boot. It fit perfectly.

Only then did the sheriff lift his gaze and stare into Longarm's face. "Your boot. Your boot heel. Boot heel found at the scene of the crime. That good enough, you bastard? You want to come quiet, or you want to do it the hard way? It's up to you."

Chapter 2

"Why don't you think with your head instead of your kneecap for five minutes, Dexter?" Longarm raged. He spoke loudly, trying to wake Chi Cochrane, who snored blissfully in his bed. "Do you think I'm stupid enough to leave a boot heel at the scene of a crime?"

The sheriff shrugged and motioned to his deputies to get behind Longarm and on either side of him. He seemed at last to be enjoying his work. He said, "I don't know how stupid you are, Long. All I know is, we found this boot heel where almost twenty thousand in gold was stole, and two men shot up. I'll just take your gun in case you figure on tryin' something else stupid."

Longarm handed over his Colt butt first. The sheriff took it. Ernie Craft said, "Don't forget the little hideout he carries, Sheriff."

"Thank you, Ernie," Sheriff Dexter said in exaggerated courtesy.

"Yeah." Ernie nodded.

Longarm shoved Ernie aside. The deputy yanked his gun up and Dexter yelled a warning. But Longarm was merely moving over to the bed to where his associate slept.

He reached over to shake Cochrane's fat shoulder with all

the rage that boiled inside him. At that instant, Wally Cochrane awoke, blinking, tasting the inside of his mouth, and gazing numbly at the sheriff and his deputies. He yawned helplessly. "My God, Lyle, what you fellows doing here this time of day?"

"We got a little trouble, Wally," Dexter said. "Looks bad. Smells bad. Might smell rotten all the way to Washington before it's over."

Scratching his belly, Cochrane stared up at Dexter. He swung his short, thick legs over the side of the bed. His torso was uncommonly long for such truncated limbs. He wriggled his feet as if trying to get the blood circulating and pushed his hands through his straw-colored hair that stood up like a clown's wig on both sides of his head. "What the hell you talking about?" he said.

Dexter gave a deprecating laugh. "I'll ask the question that Long wants asked. Reckon he was waking you up so's you could witness for him."

Cochrane grinned, half asleep. "He's a hell of a good man."

"Sure he is." Dexter's big voice dripped sarcasm. "But, was he here in this room all night?"

Cochrane yawned and nodded. "Sure he was. Far as I know."

"Far as you know?" Dexter prompted.

"Well, hell. I mean he was here. I didn't stay awake all night to be sure he was here. But every time I woke up to piss or anything, he was snoring away, right over on his bed."

"But you can't swear he was here all night?"

"What is this? I tell you, Longarm was here. What can I say? I didn't check all night."

"I know you're doing a favor for a fellow lawman, Wally," Dexter said. "I understand that. But before you say too much, I better tell you we've got some serious charges against him."

"He was here," Wally said, but his voice was less certain.

Longarm stared at the disheveled man on the bed. "Damn you, Cochrane. I woke up once and you were standing at that window staring down at the street."

"Sure, Longarm, that's right." Wally took his soiled shirt from the iron railing at the foot of his bed and slipped his arm into the sleeve. "That's true, Lyle."

"Then what?" Dexter insisted.

Cochrane shrugged. "Then I went to sleep. Hell, I was tired, trailing after Longarm all day on this case."

"I think your case has broken wide open and spewed all over your pardner, Wally. The Freedom Mine stage was robbed last night. Driver killed, man ridin' shotgun dyin'."

"Jesus Christ," Cochrane whispered.

Lyle Dexter drew a deep breath. "Now are you so bloody anxious to swear Long never left this room last night at any time?"

Cochrane buttoned his shirt over his stout belly and stood up. He shook his head. "Hell, I can't swear it, Lyle, but this is crazy. I know Longarm ain't mixed up in nothing criminal. I'd gamble my life on that."

"You say too much in his favor right now," Dexter warned, "and you might be doing just that."

Wally grinned, shaking his head. He still seemed unable to believe the big sheriff was serious. "You know damn well you can't arrest a Federal lawman, Lyle."

"You watch me," Dexter said. He held up Longarm's left boot with the heel missing. Then he held the heel out in the palm of his hand. "This here evidence talks for itself, louder'n any Federal marshal's badge. Federal marshals are just as human as the next man. They all got their price."

"Sure, most of 'em," Cochrane agreed. "But not Longarm. Hell, that son of a bitch actually lives on his hundred a month and found."

"No wonder," Dexter said, "and him puttin' away pure gold bars on the side. No. We got the evidence. Until we find some evidence contradictin' this here fact, we'll just hold the son of a bitch over in our jail."

"Don't let it throw you, Longarm," Wally said. He buttoned his pants and buckled his belt. "I'll get word right off to Billy Vail in Denver. We'll have you out of there by noon."

Dexter laughed coldly. "I wouldn't gamble on that, Wally. Nobody is likely to save this renegade's hide. He might of been able to pull off these jobs in other territories all these years and get away with 'em, but, by God, not in my county. No sir, ain't nothin' lower on this earth in my book than a lawman that's gone rotten."

Deputy Sheriff Angus Craft threw a pair of new-smelling, shining riding boots through the bars of Longarm's cell at the county jail. Longarm glanced at the boots with their pointy toes and high heels and shook his head. Still, boots were boots at the moment. Sheriff Dexter had seemed to take sadistic pleasure in forcing Longarm to walk in his stocking feet from the hotel to the lockup.

"Here's some boots for you, Long," Craft said. "Sheriff says to tell you he's keeping your boots for evidence. He says maybe you'll git 'em back in time to be hung in 'em." Craft grinned coldly. "Sheriff says to tell you these boots is better anyhow. For a real man. Not so fancy as your cavalry dress boots, but a lot more useful."

"Unless you want to walk," Longarm said. He pulled the boots on.

"Hell, you ain't walking nowhere," Craft sneered.

"That's what you fellows keep telling me."

"Sheriff says he's got you cold. Robbery, murder, betrayal of your oath—"

"You listen to the sheriff too much, Angus," Longarm interrupted. "He's working hard as he can to get in trouble. You keep on listening to him, you're going to swing with him."

The deputy sheriff gripped the bars and glared through them at the prisoner. "Now, don't you start with me, Long. Like the sheriff says, we got you."

Longarm stood up in the strange boots and exhaled heavily. He wished that Dexter had left stupid Ernie Gage to guard him. Gage was a moron; he could be bullied or scared. But Angus Craft was something else: cunning, not stupid.

He walked over to the bars. Angus Craft retreated a couple of steps, wary. "Listen, Angus. All the sheriff has got is a boot heel that was somehow planted at the scene of the robbery. That's all he's got—a heel and a head full of crap. You're a party to his hindering a deputy U. S. marshal. You got good sense. Let me out of here and I'll speak a good word for you."

"You just shut up. You ain't going nowhere. You know I wouldn't go against the sheriff."

"All I know is, you better go against him, old son, while you still can. You know the kind of prison term you can get for unlawful arrest?"

Angus Craft grinned coldly. "Naw. I don't. We ain't never had any of that kind of arrest 'round here."

Longarm held the bars, watching the deputy. "Well, you have now, Angus. Illegal arrest of a deputy U. S. marshal in the conduct of his official duties."

"You're bluffing."

"Am I? You're right, I'm just another fellow. A lawman, like you. But once the Justice Department gets on you boys' tails, it's all over for you. You're going to be miserable in prison."

"I ain't done nothin' but my duty."

"Don't tell me. Tell the Justice Department."

"I ain't tellin' nobody. I'm tellin' you. You just shut your trap and sit quiet. Sheriff says if you're innocent, you got nothin' to worry about."

Longarm grinned, displaying a cool assurance he was far from feeling inside. Anything could happen to a prisoner in Sheriff Lyle Dexter's jail, and long before the slow-moving U.S. government could act. "Oh, it's not me I'm worried about, Angus. It's you, when the officials in Denver charge you clowns with false arrest of a marshal, interfering with government officials in their duties, and obstructing justice."

"Nobody's obstructing justice. We're just locking you up so's you can't run."

"You stupid bastard. Was I running when you found me?"

"You were sleeping, because you didn't know we had the heel off'n your fancy-dan boots—"

"I was sleeping because I was here on assignment. You don't seem to catch on, Angus. This is the fourth gold shipment stolen between Golden and the U. S. Mint. This is a case I'm working on—"

"A case you *was* working on."

"You empty-headed jackass. This is a Federal investigation you're interfering with. You've locked me up in here, and the killers are getting farther away every hour."

Craft grinned at him vacantly. "One of 'em ain't. We got one. We got us a U. S. lawman that was caught red-handed. Ain't no sense you tryin' to threaten me, neither. Like the sheriff says, we're not obstructin' nothin'—the other U. S. marshal is free to investigate from hell to breakfast. Just you ain't."

"But I'm the one who's going to haunt your nightmares in the Federal pen," Longarm said.

"The hell you will." Angus Craft's voice rose, quavering. "All I know is, you kilt the guard and the driver! You robbed the gold, I didn't."

"You might as well have, Angus. You and the sheriff are going to prison, right along with whoever did pull that job."

11

Angus Craft stalked away to the front of the cell block. He flopped into a swivel chair that squealed under his weight, put his feet up on his desk, and sat picking his teeth with a thin stick. He refused to speak to Longarm or to look his way again.

Longarm saw that he had Angus thinking. The deputy sheriff's mental wheels were grinding rustily, warped from disuse.

Longarm prowled his cell. Looking at this mess with as bright an outlook as possible hardly reassured him. Golden wasn't far from Denver, but Golden's jail was as far from the outside world as Sheriff Lyle Dexter wanted it to be. If he pushed these men too far, he was well aware that he could be "killed while trying to escape" long before Chief Marshal Billy Vail could get a writ up here.

None of this made sense. On a case he had been sent to help investigate, he suddenly was the central figure on the wrong side of the law. Here he sat in jail, with circumstantial evidence calling him the killer.

A little before ten that morning, Wally Cochrane came into the cell block. Angus Craft allowed Longarm's partner to enter the corridor outside Longarm's cell.

The change in Wally Cochrane's manner toward Longarm was immediately evident. The deputy from the Chicago office grinned, but his expression was as false as a mask.

"I got a wire off early this morning, Longarm." Cochrane nodded with a little too much enthusiasm. "Yes, sir, I wired Chief Vail in Denver. Full report on this mix-up."

"Thanks, Chi."

Wally nodded and tried to smile again, but this time he failed. There was a wide gulf between them suddenly. Chi's weak smile seemed to say that he had trusted Longarm, and his partner had failed him. "Sure. We'll have you out of here in a few days, anyhow."

"A few days?" The words erupted across Longarm's lips. "What in hell did you tell Billy Vail?"

"Now, Longarm, take it easy. We're doing everything we can."

Chi stayed a few minutes longer, but conversation languished between them. Longarm said, "Have you checked the robbery and murder site?"

Cochrane seemed remote and withdrawn, almost as if he hesitated discussing official matters with Longarm. "Things are coming along," he said.

"Hell," Longarm said, "you can't ease off just because Lyle Dexter has chowder for a brain."

"Sure." Chi tried to grin and nodded. "I've been busy. But don't worry, I'm following every lead."

"Yeah," Longarm said, "but I am worried. Suddenly it's my neck I'm trusting you with."

Chi Cochrane gazed at him for a moment, uncomfortably. Then he said, "Just don't do anything stupid, Longarm. Let us handle it." He backed away, calling to Angus Craft, who unlocked the outer-corridor door. Chi gave Longarm a little salute and hurried away.

Chapter 3

From his cell, Longarm saw Sheriff Lyle Dexter come into the jail. The big lawman plodded slowly, his shoulders stooped, as if he were ill. Longarm saw the yellow sheet of a Western Union telegraph form crumpled in Dexter's hamlike fist.

Craft said something, but the sheriff only shook his head and growled sourly. Craft got up and with the heavy iron key unlocked the wide barred door. The thick-chested sheriff entered the cell block slowly, his face rigid and ashen. Craft followed him in.

"Bad news, Sheriff?" Longarm asked sarcastically.

Dexter's grizzled head jerked up and his gray eyes glittered savagely, but he said nothing. He jerked his head and Craft unlocked the cell door.

"All right, Long," Craft said. "Come on out."

"You come to your senses, Sheriff?" Longarm inquired, stepping out of the cell.

"Don't push me, Long. Far as I'm concerned, you're a thief and a murderer. As much now as when I arrested you."

"But you got the word about what it can cost you to hinder a U. S. criminal investigation, huh?"

15

"Like I say, Long, you could have a fatal accident between here and the front door. I'd regret it all to hell. But that wouldn't bring you back from the dead, would it?"

Longarm's gaze locked with the sheriff's. "You learn slow, don't you, Lyle? You're still threatening me."

"All I said was, don't push me."

Longarm gave the lawman a coyote grin. "Mind if I see the telegram?"

Sheriff Dexter hesitated a second, then shrugged. He extended the crumpled paper. Longarm straightened it and read it.

SHERIFF LYLE DEXTER GOLDEN COLORADO SUGGEST STRONGLY YOU RELEASE CUSTIS LONG ON HIS OWN RECOGNIZANCE STOP HIS EXCELLENT RECORD THIS DEPT ASSURES US GRAVE MISTAKE IN HIS ARREST STOP ARREST IMPEDES U S FEDERAL INVESTIGATION STOP THIS OFFICE GUARANTEES LONG STAYS IN GOLDEN AND COOPERATES IN YOUR INQUIRY STOP FALSE ARREST FEDERAL MARSHAL ON ASSIGNMENT EXTREMELY SERIOUS MATTER STOP RETALIATION SWIFT AND PUNITIVE STOP CHIEF MARSHAL BILLY VAIL FIRST DISTRICT COURT OF COLORADO

Longarm grinned and returned the telegram to the sheriff. Dexter looked ready to explode.

Longarm said, "If you'll just give me my hat and my guns, I'll be on my way."

"Where the hell do you think you're going?"

"Like the telegram says, Lyle, I've got inquiries to make. Robbery and murder. Remember? You've hindered me for about six hours now. That ought to be about all the time the robbers need for a clean getaway, wouldn't you say, Sheriff?"

Dexter's face flushed red to the roots of his graying hair. "You suggesting I'm mixed up in this thing?"

"What the hell, Sheriff. You don't trust me. You locked me up while the suspects got away. Why in hell should I trust you? What should I trust, Lyle? Your honest face?"

"I warn you, Long. Don't push me."

"I'll push you, Lyle. I'll push anybody I have to, to solve this case. And God help you if you are part of it."

Dexter's face purpled with rage. He clenched his fists at his sides. He managed at last to gasp, "Give gim his stuff. Get him out of here."

Longarm rode his livery-stable mount along the narrow roadway above the town of Golden. Tall pines whistled in the high winds. Ahead of him, Ernie Gage rode slowly.

Longarm smiled thoughtfully. Dexter had released him, with his Colt and his vest-pocket derringer returned to him. He had placed his flat-crowned, snuff-brown Stetson carefully on his head, dead center and tilted slightly forward, cavalry style. He felt uncomfortable in these tight new boots, but at least he was free again.

Well, almost free. Dexter had released him because he had no other choice, but he'd insisted that Ernie Gage stay with him at all times.

Lyle had grinned coldly. "For your own protection, Long."

"Aw, you're just too good to me, Lyle," Longarm had said.

"Yeah, I am, Long. This time. But I won't be if I git you back in these cells again." He watched Longarm snap the small hideout to his watch chain and place it in his vest pocket. "Oh, and Long?"

"Yeah, Sheriff?"

"Don't try any cute tricks. Ernie Gage is gonna be with you like a second shadow. And I gave Ernie orders. You try to make a break, Ernie shoots to kill."

"Yeah," Gage said.

When Longarm suggested that Ernie show him the way to the robbery and killing site, he could almost see Ernie's thought processes clanking away. Ernie tried to hold back, to let Longarm lead the way, until Longarm swore at him, "You stupid clown. Even if I knew where they robbed the stage, you think I'd be dumb enough to let you see that? Come on, lead me out there, and quit wasting time."

Ernie Gage reined in on a narrow incline between huge boulders. "This here is where they jumped the stage," he said.

Longarm nodded. "Pretty good planning. Horses slowing on the rise, narrow road, no place to go. Nothing to do but stop or fight."

"They fought," Ernie Gage said. "Both Hayes and Zembillas emptied their guns. But there's no sign any of the robbers was hit. But they sure as hell got Pete and Kaliope Zembillas—like they was clay pigeons."

Longarm shrugged. "Hell, it's easy to see. The road agents hid in the rocks and used them for cover. You people find any tracks leading away?"

Ernie Gage stared at Longarm as if the marshal were crazy. "What, horse prints? There were riders all over the place before we got out here."

Longarm nodded. He swung down and led his mount by the reins. "Why didn't you people notify Cochrane and me before you came out here?"

Ernie Gage grinned secretively and shook his head. "Hell, no time, Long."

Longarm laughed at him. "What you mean is, the sheriff's office handles its own cases its own way, and the hell with any other law enforcement."

Ernie Gage shrugged. "I don't make the rules."

Longarm spent twenty minutes climbing in the rocks on both sides of the narrow roadway. He found nothing except spent cartridges. Someone had tossed away a cigar, the kind smoked by hundreds of men.

Ernie Gage slumped in his saddle, yawning and watching him lazily. "You ain't gonna find nothin', Long. We been over all this."

"Maybe you weren't looking for the same things." Longarm returned to the roadway.

"Ready to git back to town now?" Ernie said.

"Not yet. Just relax."

He walked down the incline, going off the road at the first break in the rocks.

Ernie yelled after him, nervously, "Don't you try nothin', Long. You try to run, I backshoot you, sure's hell."

Longarm kept walking down the incline from the road. In a few minutes he heard Gage on foot, crackling through the underbrush on his trail, leading his own horse.

It took almost an hour, but Longarm finally located the place where the bandits had tied their horses.

"Three horses," he said over his shoulder to Ernie. Ernie swung down, staring at the sign in the dry creekbed, impressed. "Three horses, three sets of prints. Look, one mount has lost

18

a nail from the left front shoe. See this one? A break in the rear right shoe makes that funny pattern. And the rider don't give a shit for his animal. See here? Every shoe worn down to nothing. Horse could slip and break both their necks. This third one digs deep divots in this ordinary soil. Either a big horse or a heavy rider."

Ernie gazed at Longarm as if these deductions were a magic trick. "Hell," he whispered, "you can just about locate them horses, can't you?"

"I don't know, Ernie, but we're going to trail 'em as far as we can. Unless you'd like to ride back to Golden and wait for me."

Ernie grinned and shook his head. "No. I kinda like watchin' you. Man, you know what you're doin', don't you?"

They trailed the horsemen for almost an hour before they lost all sign. Longarm swore. He swung down from the saddle and searched the slate outcroppings in every direction.

"Shit," Ernie said, "they's got to be sign. They didn't just dissolve in thin air, did they?"

Longarm exhaled and spread his arms. "Just about. They separated here."

"But they didn't." Ernie shook his head. "They drove away in the stage. Hell, didn't Lyle tell you? They just stole the stage. Took it and left no trace."

Longarm nodded. "Then they went back for the horses after it all quieted down. Maybe only one or two went back for the horses."

"But where'd they go from here?"

Longarm glanced around in the clear afternoon sunlight. "Three different directions, likely. Maybe one went for the horses. The other two met him here. Maybe two of them took the stage, the other took the horses—the biggest man riding the big horse. The man planning this job is smart. He has a lot of experience with law officers' investigations. He figured somebody up here might trail their horses. So they met here after it was all over and just walked away."

"Son of a bitch," Ernie said.

"That just about covers it," Longarm agreed.

Longarm and Ernie returned to the Golden Hotel on the main street of the town. They didn't talk much. Longarm was chewing over the robbery in his mind.

"I'm checking into the hotel now, Ernie," he said. "You can relax. I'll let you know if I'm going to make a break."

Ernie gave him a simple-minded smile. "Reckon I'll just tag along. I want to see what you do next."

Longarm saw Wally Cochrane's gray mount napping at the hitch rail outside the hotel. The horse switched lazily at flies with its tail. Longarm reined in beside the gray. The animal sidestepped, then sagged again into lethargic rest.

Longarm stared at the ground under the gray and rubbed the flat of his hand along the horse's flank, finding the hair dry. He swore aloud and crossed the boardwalk going up onto the hotel veranda with Ernie at his heels.

They found Cochrane alone in the bar, sagging at a table. He smothered a yawn, then grinned and waved.

Longarm stood staring down at him. "What's the matter with you, Chi? You got anything to report on the murder-robbery?"

"Not a goddamn thing, Longarm. Them bastards beat us again this time."

"Maybe not, Wally," Ernie Gage said. "Longarm knows they was three of them, what horses they was riding, where they parted, and what kind of tracks their horses put down."

Wally stared up at Long. "You have been busy, haven't you, old son?"

Longarm shrugged. "I didn't find out anything more than any half-assed marshal could have done, if he'd got off his ass and tried."

"Don't get riled at me," Cochrane said. "I'm doing the best I can."

"Maybe the best you can do is one of the reasons the Chicago office transferred you down here." Longarm's voice hardened. "Maybe they were sick of you fucking off all the time."

Cochrane sat forward on his chair. "Take it easy, Long. You got a complaint about me, you make it. I'm in charge of this case."

"Yeah? Well, you're sure as hell not pushing it real hard, are you?"

"Everybody has a right to take a break, Long. Maybe I did slow down a little this morning. I mean, hell, they named you as the guilty party. That kind of slowed things down. So don't come in here tryin' to make me look bad."

"You don't need any help looking bad, Cochrane. Between

you and that fat-assed sheriff, there's been another robbery, with murder, and the trail grows colder by the hour."

"I wasted a lot of time trying to straighten things out for you, Long. You were the boy whose boot heel was found at the scene of the crime. I spent all morning trying to talk some sense into these burrheads."

"While the road agents got away with a stage loaded with processed ore."

"I know that."

"You also know this is the fourth job they've pulled. Only this one's the biggest of all. This is likely the one they've been waiting for. They get away with it, disappear, and live like kings for the rest of their lives. And you're letting them get away with it."

Cochrane shrugged and yawned again. "What the hell, Long? The miners can afford it. It ain't the end of the world, one shipment."

"Maybe the miners can afford it. I can't," Longarm said. "I never sit still for false accusations."

"Hell, we'll straighten that out. Relax."

"This is my job you're talking about. My life and the work I do."

"Yeah," Ernie Gage said. "And it wasn't just the money this time neither, Wally. I mean, two men. Pete Hayes and ol' Kal Zembillas, both dead now."

"There you are," Longarm said. "Even Ernie Gage can see it for what it is, Cochrane. It's time you got off your butt."

"Hell, I'll handle it, Long. I was just going to ride up to the Freedom Mine to talk to the owner. He thinks it was partly an inside job."

"That makes sense," Longarm said. "You want me to ride along?"

"No." Cochrane stood up and stretched. He stared into Longarm's face without smiling. "People look kind of funny at you right now. They think you might be guilty. People figure you ought to be behind bars. I'll tell you the truth, Longarm. I hate to say it to you, but I think Saltzman up at the Freedom Mine is a hell of a lot more likely to talk to me about this here case if you ain't along to upset him."

Cochrane slapped Longarm on the shoulder in an overly friendly gesture, winked at Ernie Gage, and sauntered out of the bar.

Longarm followed as far as the batwings. He stood in the shadows of the room and watched Wally ride fast, heading north out of town.

Ernie stood at his side. "Wally's got no call to talk to you like that, Longarm. He's done nothin', and at least you figured out what mounts they rode."

Longarm smiled faintly. "It ain't what Wally and I say to each other that counts, Ernie. It's what we get done."

"What you reckon to do now?"

Longarm shrugged. "I'm going to follow ol' Wally."

"Up to the mine?"

"Wherever he goes."

"You're lettin' him get a fierce start. He'll get away."

"He'll be easy to trail," Longarm said.

He counted off a long five minutes. Then he pushed open the batwings and walked out onto the hotel veranda. He glanced over his shoulder. "Why don't you stay here, Ernie? I'm not going to run away."

Ernie laughed and shook his head. "Hell, even if it wasn't my job to tail you, I'd go along. I want to see what happens."

They rode in silence for fifteen minutes on the climbing road. The loudest sounds were the deerflies, the distant thunder of dynamite at the mines, and the remote pounding at the smelter. At a fork in the road, Longarm turned left.

Ernie said, "Why you doing that, Long? The Freedom Mine is up this way."

Longarm swung down from the saddle. "I know. But Wally must be off on some other chase. He went this way."

"How do you know?"

"I've been trailing his horse. You got a rope, Ernie?"

"Yeah." Ernie loosed his rope from his saddle and tossed it to Long. "What you need that for?"

"I want to talk plain to ol' Wally."

"You plannin' to tie him up?"

"If I have to. He's not on the way to the mine, after all. And that hoofprint I been following. Take a look. See if it's kind of familiar."

Frowning, Ernie swung down from the saddle. He walked along the road searching the ground. "What do you see, Long?"

Longarm pointed to a dim outline in the road dust. "Remember those three horses we trailed this morning? Look for yourself. Remember the loose nail in the left front shoe, the mark it left? I saw that marking when I tied up next to Wally's gray at the hitch rail in front of the hotel."

Flabbergasted, the young deputy hunkered down on the road. He touched the print in the sand with his fingers. "By God, you're right," he said. "It's the same damn marking. There ain't no doubt about that."

As Ernie straightened, Longarm dropped the looped rope over his shoulders and, in record time, the young deputy sheriff lay trussed up in the road.

Ernie bit his lip. "God damn, you, Long. Why'd you do that?"

"Going to put you in the saddle, Ernie. I figure your horse will take you right back to town. You're going to be all right."

Ernie almost sobbed in rage. "I ain't never going to be all right, damn you. I trusted you, and you done this to me. Just when I was beginning to like you."

"I like you too, Ernie," Longarm said. "That's why I'm sending you back now. So you won't get hurt."

Longarm climbed through the rough country for some time. When the going got too steep and rugged for the horse, he swung down and led the animal.

On a cleared knoll, Longarm paused. He took field glasses from his saddlebag and searched the area lying before him in the overgrown hills.

He scanned east to west and then paused, bringing the glasses back and focusing in. Wally Cochrane appeared to be almost within arm's length, riding easily, unconcerned.

Longarm trailed Wally at a safe distance. He realized that Chi Cochrane was a lot smarter than he liked people to think, and cleverer than Longarm had given him credit for being. He paused frequently and reeled Wally in through the field glasses.

Wally moved as if sure that anyone who might have trailed him had lost him by now. On high crests, cramped between rocks, Longarm watched Wally until he established a pattern in his travel. Wally followed no trail very long. He kept wandering out at wide angles, yet always he drifted back north, which must be his true goal.

Crouched on the high ground, Longarm took a chance on losing Wally in the pine hammocks. He figured Wally moved gradually, but certainly north to the rugged rocky ranges above the tree line. He decided to move ahead of Wally, sweeping the high country with his field glasses.

He drew the binoculars across the spectacular ranges towering above them. The sun blazed across the western peaks and bathed the opposite sides in a purple haze. The ridges ran north and south, part of the great divide that marked the region. He dragged his gaze along the lower slopes. In the folds between the rugged peaks lay a flat and almost verdant mesa. On the table land he found the rendezvous toward which Wally rode.

Longarm held the clapboard shack, lean-to outhouse, and pine-pole corral in his sights for a long moment. He squinted his eyes against the blaze of the sun and saw two horses in the corral. They were heavy dray animals. He saw no other beings on the mesa, no sign of movement, and yet he was convinced that it was toward this desolate shack that Cochrane headed. That open field shimmered under the flat haze of the sunlight, and beyond it the ranges reared, capped with snow.

Making his decision, he returned the field glasses to his saddlebag and headed his horse down the slope and across the pine forests toward the shack on the mesa.

He rode into the clearing from the north. Leaving his mount in a grassy area concealed by boulders, Longarm studied the shack until he was certain it was vacant at the moment.

Keeping low, he ran across the clearing. The dray horses stirred, uneasy, as he ran past the corral, but there was no other movement, no sound from within the shack.

He sidled to a window on the west side, figuring to use the shack itself as a shield when Cochrane rode in from the east.

Gun drawn, Longarm moved along the wind-scarred clapboards to the window. Pushing his hat back on his close-cropped hair, he peered in through the dust-caked window.

His jaw dropped open. The single-room shack was furnished with one thing only: a dray stage marked clearly on the sides, FREEDOM MINE, GOLDEN, COLORADO.

Incredulous, he stared at the stolen stage, set at an angle across the dirt-floored shack. At last, when he convinced himself that he'd found the missing gold, he lifted his gaze and saw hinges at the rafters across the rear of the cabin. The whole back end of the hut swung up on those hinges.

As he exhaled heavily and straightened, he felt the cold, deadly pressure of a gun barrel in his neck.

Wally Cochrane's voice warned, "Just hang easy, Longarm. You'll live longer."

Chapter 4

"You had to follow me, didn't you, Longarm?" Cochrane's voice was silken-soft.

"I've been on your tail since early this morning, Chi." Still pressed against the rough clapboard shack wall, the barrel pressing into his neck just below the ear, Longarm tried to turn his head to face Wally.

The gun bit deeper. "Just stand easy, old son. We can talk like this."

"What makes you think you can get away with this, Wally?"

"This." The gun moved, pressing into Longarm's throat. "I'll kill you. Who's to testify against me?"

"Ernie Gage, for one. He knows the horse you're riding. The same horse somebody rode at the robbery and killing."

"A moron like Ernie Gage? Who'll listen to him?"

"He's a deputy sheriff."

"Hell, he couldn't get a job drivin' a honey wagon up in Chicago."

"Maybe you should have stayed in Chicago. Did you think you could come out here and make a killing outsmarting us?"

"I haven't done so bad." Wally laughed faintly. "Twenty thousand in pure processed ore. I can live pretty good on that."

25

"You'll never live good, Wally. A U. S. marshal gone rotten—do you think they'll ever let up chasing you? Sure, you can kill me, but they'll be after you like fleas. No matter how fast you run, or how far."

Wally laughed at him. "I'll take my chances. It would have been a piece of cake, but ol' Vail got suspicious of me and insisted on sending you up here too. Hell, I saw you gettin' edgy, watching me. I figured if you was in Dexter's jail, I wouldn't have to kill you. I don't want to kill you, Long, but I'm sure as hell going to have to—unless you listen to reason."

"Such as?"

"You're a smart lawman, Longarm, but you're a dumb human being. Stupid and honest. The kind that makes it tough for the rest."

"So you were rotten up there in Chicago too?"

"Oh, hell, Longarm, everybody is, one way or another. I got my appointment as a Federal marshal through my friends who were put in charge in Grant's time. I was one of the boys left over when the new people came in, so I got myself transferred to Denver—and lined my pockets with pure gold."

"You can't spend it in hell."

"Still talking like that when you're a half-inch from gettin' your brains splattered across this mesa? Get smart, Longarm, and live. Nobody'll be the wiser. When Alderman and Vought get here, we'll transfer the gold. We'll leave you tied up—and a nice bonus in the bank of your choice in Denver."

"Reckon I'll pass on it."

His breath rasping, Cochrane shoved the gun harder under Longarm's ear. His voice remained soft and urgent. "Come on, get smart for once in your life. I don't want to kill you, but I'm running out of time. Alderman and Vought will be coming up that trail any minute. When they do, your time runs out."

"I wish you had sense enough to see that your time ran out when you pried the heel off my boot and tossed it out that hotel window to some jasper down on the street. It was all over for you then, Wally. I knew nobody but you could have lifted my boot heel."

"I was trying to do you a favor. I was trying to keep from having to kill you. Listen to me, Longarm! This honesty gets you nothing. Hell, you work hard all your life, or you can play it smart for one job—this one. Hell, I've got three other shipments salted away. But this is the big one. I can pay you well—name your price."

"Beats the hell out of me, Wally. I know I got one, but I just never have figured what it is."

Wally Cochrane rammed the gun harder. "No more cheap whiskey or stinking two-for-a-nickel cheroots. Champagne and all the spangled ladies you want to drink it with you, and nobody the wiser."

"Champagne makes me sneeze."

The soft voice flicked like a whip. "On the other hand, dead men hardly ever sneeze."

The rattle of a wagon on the rocky incline to the mesa rode in on the breeze. Chi Cochrane drew in his breath in an almost agonized way. "Goddamn it, Longarm, it's Vought and Alderman. We're clearing out. For once in your stupid life, think straight. You hear 'em? The wagon? They're coming."

Cochrane's gun muzzle eased slightly as the marshal jerked his head toward the wagon trail. Wally's gun was easing back under Longarm's ear.

Longarm moved without warning. With his left hand he shoved hard against Wally's barrel chest. At the same instant he brought his right fist around and caught Cochrane just under his chin. Chi's head snapped back and he went reeling and staggering backward.

Longarm pursued him without a second's delay. He had to keep Wally from firing that gun for two reasons. Even if the shot didn't kill Longarm, it would warn Wally's confederates. And Longarm wanted them all.

Swift as a reptile, the fat marshal struck on his knees, caught his balance, and swung around, bringing the gun up, fixed on Longarm.

Longarm sent his boot toe viciously into Wally's wrist and the gun went sailing out behind them.

Cochrane lunged up from his knees and sprang at Longarm. Longarm drove his fist wrist-deep under Wally's belt buckle in a belly-jolting left. His right fist caught Chi full in the face, smashing his nose and sending him back onto his shoulders in the grass.

Longarm could hear the wagon, though he could not yet see it. He knew he had little time. This was no occasion to worry about fighting clean. He drove his boot fiercely into Cochrane's

27

crotch and the fat marshal spun over on his belly, his knees folding and jerking. He lay on the ground, twisting and sobbing into the sand.

Cochrane did not try to rise. He lay on his face, gasping for breath, his fingers digging into the dirt.

Glancing toward the trail, Longarm snagged Wally by the shirt collar and dragged him into the rocks. Cochrane's gray horse shuffled nervously as they approached.

Longarm disarmed Cochrane, tied his neckerchief into his mouth as a gag, and trussed him up across his own saddle. "Now you just lay quiet, Wally," he said. "It all ought to be over soon."

He started out of the rocks to retrieve Wally's fallen gun, but the sound of the wagon was nearer now. He didn't want to risk being spotted by Alderman and Vought. He glanced around and found a double-barreled shotgun sheathed in Wally's saddle scabbard.

He checked it, pressing the lever, finding it loaded with twelve gauge buckshot. Somehow, this felt like the equalizer he required. He dropped a couple more shotgun shells into his pocket from Wally's saddlebag.

Then he posted himself behind a couple of boulders that overlooked the mesa. The land lay silent and hot now, touched with the afternoon haze of high places. He could still hear the wagon, but there was no sign of it. The only sounds were the snuffling of the dray horses in the pine-pole corral.

He exhaled heavily, glancing over his shoulder at Wally, secured across his saddle. He sensed the tingling in his knuckles. It had felt good to hit Chi Cochrane with all the savagery and force kindled by the fires of absolute desperation. Sometimes when a man's chances were totally gone, and he had nothing to lose any more, desperation gave him the edge.

He watched the trail and the rise. Something nagged at him. Alderman and Vought were cautious; they weren't coming in without careful surveillance. Or maybe they awaited a signal from Wally.

He sweated through the longest three years of his life in the next ten minutes. He leaned against the rocks, his eyes burning and aching, not knowing whether the road agents had turned back or whether they would come in from some other direction. Maybe they'd come in from behind him. Maybe they were tracking him already. He forced himself not to turn.

The grassy country lay quiet under the westering sun—a silent white expanse with the shack dozing like an old man in the afternoon heat. Metal clinked when Wally's gray horse shook its head at the pesky deerflies; a bird chattered in a pine and was still again. And Longarm waited.

He caught his breath and held it when the flatbed open wagon, drawn by two dray horses with two saddle animals trailing from the tailgate, crested the ridge and started slowly and cautiously across the grass toward the shack.

The two men looked to come from very different segments of society. The big man wore a derby and a worsted wool suit with a high collar and tie. Only his riding boots with his trousers tufted inside them showed that he'd been riding a horse recently. The thin man wore shabby range garb and had the shifty, ferretty look of the habitual criminal who eked out a living between prison sentences. They drove the flatbad in behind the shack.

"Wonder where Wally is?" the thin little man said.

"Never mind Wally, Alderman," the big man said. "One thing for sure, Chicago Wally Cochrane can take care of himself. We'll load the wagons while we wait for him and be all ready to pull out when he gets here."

"Hot damn! Paris, France, here I come!" The thin range rider swung down from the wagon.

"Winch up the rear wall, Alderman," the big man said, getting down slowly from the wagon.

"Damn it, you don't have to tell me ever' two seconds what to do. You ain't hired me, I'm your goddamn partner, sharin' equal, and don't you forget it."

"Oh, hell, Alderman, get the wall up." Vought sounded exasperated, as if he'd gone through this argument frequently and found it less pleasurable each time.

Alderman turned a winch that squeaked as the heavy lines inched through pulleys, lifting the entire back wall of the shack even with the break of the roofing.

Longarm watched the two men transfer the boxes of processed ore from the stage inside the shack to the flatbed. The wagon had a false bottom, which Vought removed, and they placed each box carefully into the wagon bed.

Longarm grinned faintly, seeing that Vought permitted Alderman to transport two boxes to each one of his. He figured Vought as the inside man from the Freedom Mine, the brain behind the robbery.

He heard Alderman's high voice across the grass. "We really going to burn this shack and the stage?"

"We really are, Alderman, soon as Wally gets here."

Alderman shook his head. "Don't sound too smart to me. My ol' grandpa always used to say you jest cain't hide smoke on a mountain."

Vought gazed along his nose at the thin, sun-dried man. "The very fact that you oppose burning this evidence assures me with greater certainty than ever that it is indeed the wisest course—the only course."

"You're a smart-talking bastard, Vought." Alderman glanced around the mesa. "Be happy when Wally gets here. Be even happier when we're clear of this country and make our final divvy. That's the day I'm looking for, the last time I have to look at your ugly face or listen to your stuck-up voice."

"Just load the gold," Vought told him.

"That's it," Alderman said, "it's all loaded."

Longarm moved out from behind the rocks in one fluid motion. He held the gun out high before him where they could see it. His yell rattled against the overhanging ridges and bounced back, a mocking echo.

"Stop! Hold it right there."

Both men froze in their tracks, but they were old hands at crime; they reacted instantly. They were pulling their guns from their holsters as they spun around to face Longarm crossing the grass at a run.

As they brought their guns up, Longarm shot them, the twelve-gauge roaring like thunder and lightning. Vought and Alderman went staggering back, dead before they struck the ground.

Longarm stalked to where the road agents lay. The horses shuddered and whickered nervously. He replaced the false bottom in the flatbed. Then he hefted Alderman's body and dumped it into the wagon. Vought was heavier. He knelt, lifted the heavy body on his shoulder, and levered himself to his feet. Vought landed with a resounding thump beside the skinny little range rider.

Longarm tied the dray horses to the rear of the tailgate along with the saddle animals. Then he brought the gray with Cochrane tied across the saddle and secured it.

He looked around, exhaling heavily. When he brought in his own mount, his chores were finished.

He felt rotten, and he couldn't even say why. He swung up onto the wagon and headed to the trail back to Golden. Maybe he was sick because Chicago Wally Cochrane had been a fellow marshal. It didn't help any to tell himself that Wally was a conscienceless rascal and always had been. Wally represented the cream of poor old U. S. Grant's crime-riddled administration. And the reprobate Cochrane had not only failed Longarm on this job; he'd framed him, betrayed him, and would have let him die.

It helped a little to think he'd cleaned up a bad mess. It ought to be worth a kind word if not a commendation from Billy Vail. He'd settle for a few days' rest. That was the least he could expect from Billy. He grinned faintly, looking forward to his return to Denver.

Chapter 5

Billy Vail wore a black funeral band of mourning on the left sleeve of his pongee shirt.

Longarm stared at his boss. He had sauntered in this morning expecting a commendation of some sort, or at least a reluctant suggestion that he take a day or two off and get some rest. He grinned wryly. This was the least he'd anticipated but, from long experience, he should have known better.

From the moment Longarm had pushed open the outer door, neatly lettered in gold leaf, UNITED STATES MARSHAL, FIRST DISTRICT COURT OF COLORADO, he had sensed tension.

He paused just inside the door, instinctively sniffing at the uneasy atmosphere in the suite of offices. He shrugged. He'd been around long enough to know that discontent, malcontent, and disruption were almost to be counted on. Still, he had recently come up out of a hellish situation and he expected more.

The pink-cheeked young clerk looked up from his newfangled typewriter and jerked his head nervously toward Billy Vail's inner sanctum. "The chief has been looking for you for the past two hours. I think I'd better warn you. He's most upset."

"He got upset from his mother's milk." Longarm shrugged and crossed the small, compactly furnished outer office to the inner door.

The young clerk leaped to his feet. "I'd better tell him you've arrived."

"Why?" Longarm frowned. "He knew I'd get here sooner or later."

Seeing that he was unable to intercept Longarm at the door, the young clerk sighed and sank back into his pinewood swivel chair. It squeaked loudly. "It's just that he's very upset," he said, "and he always hollers at me when we don't run things according to the book around here."

"I'll put in a word for you," Longarm promised. He'd opened the door, grinning, and stopped, stunned at the sight of Billy Vail's anguished face and the black armband on his sleeve.

Vail's hands were full of papers. When he saw Longarm, he set the stack of correspondence down on the other piles of bulletins and despatches that swamped his desk top. As Longarm well knew, all of it was marked URGENT.

As Vail retreated behind the desk, Longarm caught the arm of the red morocco chair that was the single piece of comfortable furniture in the office, and pulled it around to facing his boss. He sagged deep into the chair, studying Vail. The chief marshal looked so miserable that Longarm refrained from remarking on his appearance.

Vail stood for some moments behind his desk without speaking. At least fifteen years older than Longarm, Billy Vail had hunted down and dragged in his share of outlaws. In his day he had ranged over most of the western states and territories and often across the Rio Grande into Mexico. But his day was past as far as guns and saddles and shootouts were concerned, and nobody hated this more than the chief marshal. Time had snagged him down to his big littered old desk.

Longarm settled himself in the upholstered chair and chewed his unlit cheroot, grinning faintly. Billy was desk-bound, but he wore his ill-healed wounds like hammered medals from past violence in almost forgotten places. These settlements were cleaner, better places to live because Billy Vail had once stopped there, his guns blazing. Only one enemy was too tough for Billy: age. Age had promoted him out of harm's way. Losing his hair, going to flab from too much desk time, he was a tough man growing reluctantly old. He expected his men to match his record and, when they couldn't, to hang up their spurs.

Vail said finally, "Too many men try to hang on to jobs like this when they're too goddamn old."

"You plannin' to retire, Chief?" Longarm asked.

Vail's head jerked up. "What the hell do you mean? I'm not talking about me. Anybody could handle this job. I'm talking about men on the line—men like you."

"You're right, Chief. I feel older than God this morning."

"And I'm not talking about you, either. Don't worry, Long, when I see you slowing down, getting cautious, or creaking in your joints, the first one you'll hear it from will be me."

"You're too damned good to me, Billy."

"That's right. I would be doing you a favor, Long. Your job is no job for an aging man, a cautious man, or a worried man. It really ain't a fit profession for a married man, either, though there have been a few—damned few—good lawmen who were husbands and fathers. On the trail is no place to be worried about the little lady back at the house, and what will become of her and the children if a bullet finds its way into your gut."

"You're in a hell of a sweet mood this morning, Billy."

"I'm just looking at life the way it is." Billy stared at Longarm, scowling. "A death does that to you sometimes. It makes you take a good look at life and how much of it you got left—and what you've done with it—and what it's done to you."

"Sour stomach," Longarm suggested.

"What the hell you talking about?"

"Sour stomach. It causes you to feel low. Drags you down so you hate everybody, and life, and nothing looks worth a damn. Lime water and soda mint will fix you up."

Billy Vail swore. "I'm not sick. My belly is no more sour today than any other day. Damn it, a fine old friend of mine has been killed, and I'm torn up about it. Gut sick."

Longarm exhaled heavily and waited. He glanced about Billy's austere government bureaucrat office. Vail's grade didn't rate a carpeting on the floor, but he was permitted three chairs: one swivel, one straight, and the red morocco guest armchair—you never knew when some high-ranking official might drop in with a request or complaint or demand—and two cabinets. A single window opened on the plaza. An American flag and clock shared wall space with a map of the western half of the United States and a fresh formal photograph of the President.

"Harry Varner got it," Vail said, his voice cracking slightly. "Son of a bitch was gunned down."

"Harry Varner?" Longarm sat forward in the chair. It always was gut-clutching when another marshal was killed.

"That's right, Deputy U. S. Marshal Harry Varner. Gunned down by some bank robbers when he walked in on them during a holdup. The hell of it is, the poor bastard was down there in Galveston on a vote fraud investigation. I reckon you've noticed—along with most of the rest of the deputies—that I've been keeping Harry out of the rough stuff for the past few years."

Longarm shrugged. "It was nothing to me. I knew Harry was married, over forty, and getting fat. I didn't care what you did with him, as long as you didn't send him out on a job with me."

Billy Vail looked ill. "I'd never have done that, Long. Not to you. And not to Harry. I should have come down hard on him. I should have demanded his retirement. But he had a family and he needed every damned dime."

"Harry Varner." Longarm sighed and shook his head again.

"I been gut sick, Long. Ol' Harry was a friend of mine from the old days. Wasn't a better man to side you in the business. He was some younger than me, but I've sat on my ass in this office and watched Harry get old, get married, and get saddled with children. I feel almost like I killed him."

"That don't make sense, Chief."

"Grief don't always make sense, Long. All I know is that if I had been less a friend of Harry's and more the kind of chief marshal Washington expects me to be, Harry would be alive on a little spread somewhere—"

"And choked to death on a chicken bone. You can't say how or when a man is going to die, Billy."

"At least, if I'd made Harry retire, even if he died accidental, he'd've been in the bosom of his family, with his loved ones around him, not down in the ass-end of Texas, walking in on a bank holdup."

"Stop feeling like it's your fault, Billy. It won't help a damn thing. It won't bring Harry back."

"I ain't thinking about bringing Harry back. I ain't even really thinking about the job of taking his things and the government settlement check to his widow. No, I'm full of rage, Long. I'm thinking about burning those sons of bitches that got Harry."

"You? Personally?" Longarm sat forward in his chair. He was beginning to realize how deeply moved Billy Vail was.

"Me." A small muscle worked in the hard line of Vail's jaw. "Personally." He stared at his clenched fists. "Hell, I feel I owe it to Harry—and to his Mildred."

"What the hell is it going to prove, to get yourself killed?"

"I'm not trying to prove anything, Long. It's something inside me. I wronged Harry Varner, and I need to right that wrong, if I'm going to be able to live with myself."

"You're letting sorrow foul up your thinking, Billy."

"Am I? I don't think so. What do you know about losing the kind of friend you owe your life to—not once or twice, but many times over? How many times did Harry and I try to drink the saloons dry down along the border? When I think of all the times trouble sneaked up and got me by the gullet and I looked over my shoulder to see ol' Harry standing there like some avenging angel. The kind of friendship Harry and I had was built up over the tough years on the back trails and in the bad towns."

Longarm shrugged. "I figure if ol' Harry could speak to you, Billy, he'd tell you he was as deep in your debt as you ever were in his. I'll lay you odds it evens out. He stayed on the job. Maybe he stayed too long, but it was his decision. And he paid for it."

"You miss the point, Long. I let him stay. I let him stay and get killed."

"You let him do what he wanted to do. For all we know, maybe Harry went out just the way he'd've wanted. He didn't want to rust, Billy."

"Those bastards killed him, and they got away with it."

"They haven't got away with it. Not yet. The Texas Rangers will be on their tails."

Billy Vail swore. "The Texas Rangers were on their tails. They tracked them as far as the Big Thicket, that swamp land in eastern Texas. South of what they call the Piney Woods country and bordered on the west by a huge open savannah called the Post Oak Belt. This swamp reaches to the Sabine River and then becomes the bayous of Louisiana. A gang of men can lose themselves just about as long as they like in the Big Thicket."

"Are the Rangers still trailing them?"

"Not really. It's still an open case with the Rangers, and I'm not faulting them in any way. They're a great bunch of men, trying to do a hell of a job with too few deputies. Ain't their fault they got to cover the whole state with a handful of overworked guns."

"What happened?"

"What happened is what that gang of thieves must have counted on happening. They outran the law to the Big Thicket, and they lost themselves in there with a fortune in currency."

"They all got away?" Longarm asked.

"As a matter of fact, the Rangers were able to close in on Haggerty's gang—" Billy Vail began.

"Haggerty?" Longarm interrupted.

"Blast Haggerty. They say he's like a riverboat gambler, with Old South manners, a slick way of dressing, and the mind and morals of a weasel. He's smart, and he masterminded the job. He's the son of bitch I want—the one that makes me want to step down from this desk and go on the prowl one more time."

"Don't be a fool, Billy." Longarm spoke quickly, to get Vail's mind off his vengeance plan. "You say the Rangers closed in on Haggerty's gang?"

"They shot and killed a couple of them on the run. Shit, I'll wager you that was all in Haggerty's plan. He knew how many he'd lose. He knew all the odds, and he knew he'd lose himself in the swamp."

"How do you know he's lost in the swamp?"

"It's all right here in this goddamn report," Billy Vail said. "The Rangers followed Haggerty's bunch into the thickets. But the Rangers gave up when their horses started to drown under them. They came to this place where they could tell Haggerty loaded his men and horses into pirogues—those are big boats that look like dugout canoes—and simply disappeared into the jungle. They figured the outlaws might try to cross the Thicket and the Sabine River, so they sent telegrams to the authorities in Louisiana. No sign of them. And that's where they had to give up. Goddamm it, they gave up and Haggerty lives—with all that money—and he killed Harry."

"All it means is that Haggerty is hiding out for now. Hell, Billy, that don't mean it's over."

Vail smashed his clenched fist down onto the desk. "You're goddamn right it ain't over. And it won't be over until I've got that bastard Haggerty's gizzard in my right fist. Only Haggerty don't know that. He figures every angle, right down to how many men he'll likely lose before he makes it to freedom. But one thing he didn't take into account, and that was that he killed my friend Harry Varner."

"It'll work out."

"You're goddamn right it'll work out. Maybe Harry wasn't the best marshal on the payroll anymore. Maybe he was damned near the worst. No, the worst was your man Chicago Wally Cochrane."

"Chi wasn't my man, Billy. You assigned him."

"He was one of the old bunch from the last administration. I smelled something wrong about him from the day they transferred him here from Chicago. But a marshal that goes bad is the worst. Harry wasn't like that. Harry was—"

"Just incompetent."

"Incompetent, hell. He had brushes with death that would have scared the shit out of you. I admit he had slowed down plenty. Too much. He was cautious, never took chances, missed clues as big as his head. He didn't really think straight anymore. But I figured the government owed him. He was the kind of guy that never made headlines, but he helped make something out of this wild country. I figured the government owed him," Billy Vail repeated.

"Nobody can fault you for that, Billy."

"I can. I let him hang on. I tried to give him easy jobs, tried to protect him. But I killed him."

"You're not thinking straight."

Vail glared at him across the desk. "What do you know about a friend being killed? Nothing. By God, Harry was maybe my best friend on this earth. Closer than any brother. And I don't mean to let Haggerty and those other sons of bitches who killed Harry get away with it and all that loot. No, sir. It sticks in my craw."

"Do I get the feeling you're about to assign me to East Texas?"

"I want them bastards, Long. If I have to resign this job and strap on a gun myself."

Longarm laughed. "That would be the worst way in the world to try to get them." He stirred in his chair. "Has it occurred to you, Billy, that there's a hell of a good chance

Haggerty and his men and the loot are long gone from the Big Thicket by now?"

"Some of the Rangers say that in this report."

"Then sending anybody down to the Big Thicket would be kind of a waste of time, wouldn't it?"

"I told you, I'm ready to go myself."

Longarm spread his hands. "Oh, hell, I'll go. I just want it on record that it looks like a waste of time to me and to some Texas Rangers who know that country better'n we do."

"My instinct tells me they're still in the Thicket. Haggerty is rat-smart. Where would he be safer than in trackless wastes that are too wet to walk and too dry for most boats? It's a place where a man can get hopelessly lost in fifteen minutes. No, the bastard is in there, laughing at the bankers in Galveston, at the Texas Rangers, and at poor Harry, who blundered in on them. Well, by God, I won't have them laughing."

Longarm exhaled heavily. "When do you want me to leave?"

Vail shook his head and prowled his office like a caged animal. "I got no idea what I'd be sending you into—"

"But that don't stop you—"

"I can send some men with you. You can hire guides down there."

Longarm stood up. "Don't send anybody with me. I can see that stalking into trackless swamps is kind of like suicide and kind of stupid. But I work best alone."

Billy Vail almost smiled through the grief on his face. "Yeah. You do move sudden and unexpected-like. Hard for a partner to keep up with."

"That's the way it is."

"And you don't like to tell anybody in advance what your plans are."

"You got to chew the apple one bite at a time."

Vail shook his head. "That's why I never have tried to find you a steady partner, Long. That would be a chore that'd just be beyond me. It would be almost impossible, even if this Denver office could stand more than one such ornery cuss as you.

"And I can tell you this. The Texas Rangers will approve of you coming in down there. It isn't they don't feel capable of wiping their own asses, but they think maybe a new broom— you—would sweep cleaner."

"And no skin off their noses if I happen to step into quicksand in the Big Thicket."

"Not a shred. I do want to go on record, though, as trying to send another marshal, or even a team of marshals, with you. I don't want you in over your head. This case is important to me, and I want it handled right."

"Well, you keep on working by the book, Billy, and I'll do it my way, as long as I can."

"I know, Longarm. And I know if anyone can catch those bastards, you will."

"I'll do what I can. Alone. You sent me out with a partner last time, name of Wally Cochrane. Wally not only nearly got me killed—he damned near killed me himself."

Vail nodded. "I been wanting to say, Long, you handled that business well. You did a good job. But good ain't damn near enough for this Haggerty bunch. I'll mark this here case closed when you bring me Haggerty's big toe."

Chapter 6

Longarm cursed the heat of Galveston island.

After the mile-high thin air of the Colorado high country, Longram felt as if he'd tumbled down a rathole into an alien world.

Galveston wasn't even really an island. It was more of a sandbar, one of the scores of narrow barriers whose dunes rise like parapets against the sea. Crossing the intercoastal waterway via paddle-wheel ferry, Longarm saw the sky blanketed by screeching, whirling, wheeling, chattering birds: hungry seagulls mostly, with a few pelicans and terns attracted like curious onlookers at some maritime disaster.

When he stepped off the short-run stage in front of the Galveston Hotel, he noticed that the town was beginning to show the flamboyant signs of a wealthy invasion. Rich Yankees were erecting the monstrous castles overlooking the lime-colored sea. He'd expected a backwater town, but he was wrong. Even in the late afternoon of an inclement day, the town was bustling with life, loud with activity. Hump-backed mountains of seagoing coal marked the shipping docks along the waterfront.

Dusk was gathering on this damp, rainy afternoon. Coal-oil lamps glowed in wispy gray mists. Along the piers, vessels from every land lay to: keelboats, flatboats, and paddle-wheelers from the rivers strung beside hulking barges, trawlers, seagoing freighters, and cattle boats. The seacoast smell of salt and fish and mud rose to mix with the odors from the brigs: coffee from Colombia, cattle and hides from the Texas plains, lumber, rum, and tar.

On both sides of the shell-paved main street clapboard wooden shacks clustered beside more solid structures: gingerbread, bay-windowed, gabled white seaside inns with long shaded front porches reflecting the sun, boasting wide, tall windows through which errant breezes sauntered, gamboled, or ran riot. Saloons and Mexican eating places offered ale and raw oysters, clams, mussels, mullet, catfish, shrimp, and snails in every kind of sauce. Around him rose the din of a score of languages and dialects as Mexican peddlers, Spanish sailors, Norwegian, English, and Arabian seamen all tried to be heard above the shouting twang of Texan and Kentucky drawls and Yankee tenors. Too tired to take in the confusion of all these establishments and all these people, Longarm stepped into the hotel lobby. Tomorrow would be soon enough to start on the already cold trail of the Haggerty gang.

Longarm walked in the warm sun toward the dazzlingly white stretch of endless beach. The sun braised his shoulders; there was no hint of breeze, just moist humidity from the sea.

Two days in Galveston hadn't bought him very much; nothing he could put in an official report. But at last he had learned of a man who was very familiar with the Big Thicket, and might be willing to act as Longarm's guide.

He found the clapboard shack he sought, a tarpaper-roofed hut set on the dunes above the beach. A hound slumbered under the slab step. The front door was closed but all the windows stood open, their curtains hanging like sails in dead calm. He heard no sound from within the one-room house. The chickens in their pens pecked silently, and trapped armadillos, raccoons, and rabbits panted in their wire-faced cages.

Longarm rapped on the door and waited. A man's voice, slightly strained, called in a Mexican accent, "Come on in. Door's unlocked."

Longarm pushed open the door and stepped into the shadowed room. For a brief instant he was blinded after the blaze of sunlight. As his vision slowly returned, his eyes focused on the two figures on a narrow bed under one window. The man sitting on the bed was almost as big as Longarm, and his bare chest was the color of brightly polished mahogany. He wore a pair of Levi's and his feet were bare.

The tiny Mexican girl was completely naked. Her dark-brown hands, with their long and slender fingers, gently stroked the man's back. Her long black hair draped over the man's bare arm and shoulders. The girl moved her hand up to soothe his thick black cap of hair. Her legs were apart and the dark mound at her thighs gleamed damply. Her narrow waist was flat and flared to beautifully rounded hips and shapely legs. Her creamy breasts lay like two small hillocks on her chest, crested with dark rubies.

Longarm tried politely to avert his gaze, but there was little to look at in the room: a pinewood table, a cook stove, a couple of straw-bottomed chairs, clothing hanging upon pegs in the bared wall studs. Longarm was glad he hadn't knocked on the door ten minutes earlier or, he was sure, he'd have interrupted them.

Glancing at Longarm for the first time, the man saw his discomfort. "What the hell," Capo said, "it's all right, mister. Look at Leona if you want to. Every other man on this island does."

The girl snarled from the bed, "You lie, Capo."

"It's true," he said, jerking his head around.

"I do what I have to," she said from the bed. "I do what I have to, Capo."

"You don't believe me?" Capo said to Longarm. "You fuck her. Go ahead, if you want to."

Longarm spread his hands. "Maybe some other time. I don't like to mix pleasure with business."

Capo stared at him. "I never will understand you white men. I hope I never have that much business, eh, Leona?"

"You go to hell, Capo," she said. She closed her legs and turned onto her side, facing the wall. In less than a minute, Leona was fast asleep, breathing deeply.

Longarm and Capo sat on the front stoop of the shack, in a patch of shade. A soft, salty breeze cooled his face. Capo said, "You didn't come down here to screw Leona. What are you looking for?"

"You."

45

"What you want?" Capo asked. "I don't kill. I mean, maybe if somebody offered me enough cash I *might* kill. But you don't look like you could afford it."

"Somebody told me you know the Big Thicket."

Capo's dark face came up and he stared at Longarm. "I might have known. You're the *hombre* going around asking everybody about Blast Haggerty. You tryin' to git yourself killed?"

"Not particularly. Getting killed is a risk I take. I'm a U. S. marshal."

Now Capo's dark face pulled into a savage smile. "A real U. S. marshal, huh? So you're gonna march into the Big Thicket and drag ol' Blast Haggerty out by the ass?"

"I'm going to try. That's why I'm here; I want to hire you."

"I don't go against Blast Haggerty or his gang. You got the wrong boy. Capo is a peace-loving man, half-nigger, half Mexican-Indian. I got the beauty from all the races, and I got all their good sense. A man wants money bad enough to kill for it, he can keep it. That's the way ol' Capo feels."

"I don't want you to kill. I do my own gun work. I want a guide, somebody who really knows that country up there."

"Hell, mister, who knows the Thicket? Some know parts of it, others know other parts."

"I want the part Blast Haggerty and his gang are holed up in."

"You want horns, mister, but I reckon you're going to die butt-headed. I can guide you. I've been in there many times and I've always come out alive. It ain't that I know the whole Thicket—nobody knows that, except maybe a few ol' bull alligators. What I got is one hell of a sense of direction. I can tell you north, south, east, and west on the blackest night in the deepest forest. I don't know how I do it. A keen sense of direction. That's what a man gets when he hires Capo."

"How much?"

"I get two dollars an hour, mister. Twenty-four dollars a day, every day."

"Jesus. No wonder you don't work much."

"I work enough. I don't git paid for what I do, mister. When I guide you, I don't do much of anything except get you in there and get you out. But with you looking for Blast Haggerty, you might have to leave my pay at the bank in advance."

"I can arrange that. I hope my boss will believe me when I quote your price."

"Hell. Tell him, you want the best, you pay for the best. I'm paid for what I know."

"When can you leave?"

Capo shrugged. "A few days to get supplies laid in, and we'll need horses and a light pirogue for two that a horse can carry. After that, you let me know a night in advance. I can screw Leona enough to last me until I get back." Capo sighed heavily. "Hell, I know it won't keep Leona satisfied till I get back, but I can't expect miracles."

From inside the house they heard Leona's savage cry. "You lie, Capo! You lie! I can wait just as long as you can."

Chapter 7

Longarm and the halfbreed Capo left the small riverboat on the Trinity River at the site of an abandoned logging camp. The "cut and move on" motto of the lumbermen for nearly thirty years in the Big Thicket country had left vast and desolate scars in the virgin forests.

Leading their horses and pack mule, they crossed the clumsily butchered clear-cut area, a graveyard of stumps cringing under patches of briars, weeds, and grass. The sun blazed mercilessly on the sodden mud. The horses' hooves sank into the mire and came free with sucking sounds.

The forest spread toward them, as if trying to reclaim the scarred region. Once they entered the hardwood hammock the sun was blocked out except in brief glinting shafts in the thick feathering of tall white and red oaks, hickories, and magnolias. The Big Thicket got almost as much rain as any rain forest, and its trees grew to incredible sizes, rearing tall and blotting out the skies.

After the open places and the river, this thick, forested land cast a strange and powerful spell. The heat was intense; there was not a whisper of breeze. The silence closed in on them, blanketing off the rest of the world.

Longarm said, "I can see how a man could get lost. It's even hard to breathe in here."

"Hell, this is the good part," Capo said over his shoulder. "This is the hardwood forest. Wait till we hit the sloughs and the salt marshes."

When he stopped talking there was no resonance of his voice, as if he'd never spoken. Longarm had the eerie feeling that if he yelled the matted trees would muffle his shouting and fling it back at him. He held his breath, listening for any sound in the deathlike stillness. Sun streaks glittered briefly, intensifying the shadowy, mossy gloom.

They moved soundlessly over the damp carpeting of rotting leaves, spread like compost under the beeches, maples, cedars, elms, and live oaks.

Capo said, "This is the place to make up your mind. You can always turn back. I figure there's no better time than now. We can go back to the river and wait for a downstream paddle-wheeler. The deeper we go, the harder it is to turn back—or even to find your way back."

"I thought you knew this country."

"I tol' you, nobody knows this country. It changes. It stays the same all the time and it changes all the time."

"You sound worried."

"I sound like I got good sense. I tell you, hunters traveling in here in groups have plain vanished in this unmapped wilderness. Nobody ever even found their bones."

"Anybody ever go looking for them?"

Capo laughed without mirth. "You're jokin', ain't you?"

They moved deeper, the forest closing in tighter upon them, the trees strung and matted together by vines and briars. With machetes, they made paths for their horses and themselves through buckeye, willows, and tall grass. They lost the sun and the sky for eternal moments in tunnel-like brush. The silence deepened. No breeze could thrust its way through the tangle of trees and undergrowth. Distantly, the dominant trees reached up, as if gasping for breath, and their far-away soughing intensified the hot stillness.

Capo said, "You know what you're looking for?"

"Why?"

"Well, hell, I thought it would be a good idea if we both knowed what we're looking for. That way we can recognize it if we see it."

"Settlements."

"What kind of settlements?"

"Where a man—or men—could hide out."

Capo laughed faintly. "God knows there are plenty of those. Settlements populated with backwoodsmen who hate strangers like poison."

"Still, Haggerty and his gang are in here, hiding. Someone's taken them in."

Capo shrugged. "We'll keep looking. It's your ass. But I can tell you one thing. Ain't nobody goin' to say one word to you about Blast Haggerty. Hell, in Galveston they were real talkative compared to what you're going to find up here."

"Sound like real nice folks."

"They live one way—their way. That means you leave them alone, and they leave you alone." Capo laughed. "Unless you got something they want."

"If Haggerty is in here, I have to try and find him."

"All you'll find in here is marshes and forests. Towns where people would rather kill you than talk to you. Places where a man could be hidden ten feet from you, and you'd never find him. See what a job is ahead of you?"

"I never thought it would be easy."

Capo whistled, amazed. "I tell you, you white men just tear it right off the trees. Your brains ought to tell you, it's an impossible job. But you go charging on."

"All I ask is a chance. Haggerty and his bunch got in here. They're still in here."

"Unless they caught a riverboat on the Sabine to the Gulf, and took off to Europe to spend their money."

"They're looking for them in every civilized area between here and New Orleans."

"They might be dead."

Longarm shrugged. "They might be. But, what the hell, you still collect your two dollars an hour, don't you?"

Capo laughed. "I just hate to see you waste your money, that's all."

Though Longarm couldn't judge by looking any distance— he couldn't even see the sun, except for bright patches glinting infrequently in the tallest trees—he figured they were walking down an eternal, gradual incline.

Capo pointed out an ivory-billed woodpecker and Longarm stared at the bird, incredulous. Its ivory-white bill, deep-black and snow-white feathers, and red crest, and its body, larger than a crow's, made it a brilliant sight, an exotic species, picking at insects in the wet tree trunks where wild orchids grew between poison ivy and long strands of gray moss.

Distantly, a panther wailed and fell silent. A deer streaked across the underbrush ahead of them, soundless in the furtive quiet.

"Comin' on to marshes," Capo said. "Maybe the sight of them inlets, an inch deep and ten miles long, will turn you back."

"Why are you so anxious to turn back?"

Capo grinned at him, his bronzed face twisted in a taunting smile. "I know you're a U. S. marshal, but there must be a better way to earn a living than this."

Longarm grinned back at him and shrugged. "It's all I know."

Capo paused at the brink of what looked like an impassable lake of grass and let Longarm look over the obstacles ahead. The grass glistened in the sun, its sharp edges razor-keen. Small, narrow lanes of water twisted through the carpeting of grasses. Distantly, across it, willows and elms marked the first layer of high ground—or perhaps it was only an island in the sea of grass. Above the line of willows, dogwood flowered, along with bay and holly trees. Over it all, so dark as to appear an impenetrable green, reared tall pines.

"That's where we're headed." Capo nodded, indicating the dry land. "You ready to call it impossible now?"

"How do we get there?"

"We walk careful, lead the horses slow, and pray a lot."

"You want to lead the way?"

"That's what you're paying me for."

Capo led his horse and the pack mule out into the grass. Water and mud seeped up around his boots. He gave Longarm a grin. "Water moccasins don't usually bite unless they're sheddin' or riled up or just feelin' ornery."

Longarm led his horse out into the grass. Capo swore at the mule and the thick-bellied animal moved forward reluctantly.

"I think in places like this, mules are probably a hell of a lot smarter than horses and us," Capo said. "It's like being blind—you hear better. Or deaf—you see better. The dumber you are, the sharper your instincts. Now this ol' mule knows we're crazy going out into this. His instinct tells him what dangers there are — moccasins, quicksand, deep holes, drop-offs."

"You talk a lot," Longarm said.

"When I'm scared," Capo said, "I like to hear the sound of my own voice."

The tallest grasses brushed hard against Longarm's legs, cutting like knives into his pants and the skin beneath. They tried walking along the narrow waterway paths, but they were treacherous. Brown water rolled along between the grasses over white sand bottoms, and the open ways meandered through blue bonnets, sneezeweed, and prairie grass.

"When we get up into the high ground," Capo said. He swore and laughed as a five-foot moccasin slithered from the brown water into the high grass near his legs. "If we get up on high ground, we'll find some pawpaws and chinaquin nuts. You ever eat chinaquin nuts?"

"I don't think so."

"They're so good they ought to cost ten dollars an ounce," Capo said.

They climbed up the steep slope, pushing through willows and elms toward the pines and hickories on the ridge. Longarm sagged on an open incline in the sun, drying his legs. Capo gathered up nuts and berries.

They sat in the stillness, eating the wild berries. Longarm agreed the chinaquin nuts were delicious, though it was almost impossible to get them out of their hard, sticky burrs.

He watched Capo pull a crude penciled map from his knapsack. The big, mahogany-brown man spread out the paper and studied it. "We ought to make it by nightfall," he said at last.

"Make what?"

"Settlement called Clayville. It's on one of the rivers through the Thicket. It's the first place you're going to find people who aren't going to tell you about Blast Haggerty. They won't give you the time of day if they can figure some way to help it."

They had climbed in the soft dry sand of the pine hammock for only a few minutes when they reached the crest which snaked along in a ridge north and south in the wilderness.

As they started down the slope, a silence unlike anything they'd encountered so far seemed to float about them.

At the foot of the incline they waded out through dwarf

palmettos into waist-deep water. They met their first alligators, some of them fifteen feet long, sunning on logs, gliding into the brown water, and disappearing among the cypresses and water tupelos.

They left the palmettos, tupelos, and maples and entered the dead, becalmed world of the cypress swamps. Though the sun still shone and the humidity was unbearable, there was an atmosphere of dark and silent water waste, a hot, lifeless slough. It was a place of unnerving silences and sounds, the squeal of small, skittering animals. Mink, otter, raccoon raced along submerged logs and spun out into the black waters, making hardly a ripple, sending up only the faded whisper of sound. Occasionally they would hear a muffled outcry of pain or terror, or the faraway whoop of cranes.

They moved into the shallows and inlets, reflecting sodden fern and limp-hanging Spanish moss. The marshes stretched eternally, a world of decay. The trees stood brown and dead in the black water, and the water lay motionless under the sullen canopies of bared limbs entwined with vines against the sky.

"Is it like this all the way to Louisiana?" Longarm wondered, his voice low.

"Who knows?" Capo said.

"Haven't you ever been here before?"

"Probably. But all these swamps look alike. You just keep moving and keep hoping."

"Hoping?"

Capo laughed. "Hoping that you can keep moving. People have drowned in here from plain old exhaustion a few hundred feet from dry ridges."

"This silence gets to you."

"You better get used to it, mister. It's the same or worse through the whole Thicket. People used to open spaces turn into screaming madmen in here."

"You got any idea how far it is to Clayville?"

"Nope. We hit a ridge, we head left. If we come to a creek big enough to support the little riverboats that go deep into the interior, we ought to find a settlement. One of them might even be Clayville."

"You're one hell of a guide."

"Worth every penny. I got you in here and I'll get you out.

Little things like whether we find Clayville on the first try or the tenth don't count."

They laughed together in the stifling silence.

Longarm heard Capo's long exhalation, as if the halfbreed were breathing for the first time in ten minutes. "Yonder," Capo said, "a ridge. We can make a little campfire, dry out our clothes and boots. Maybe we can kill a rabbit or a couple of doves. We'll feel a hell of a lot better with our stomachs full."

"Sounds good," Longarm said.

Capo laughed, coming out of the swamp and staggering on the rim of the dry incline. "I hope you can cook."

Exhausted, Longarm stood at the edge of the swamp. He watched Capo lead the saddle horse to dry land. He had more trouble trying to pull the mule out of the deep water than he'd even had trying to force the animal into the bog.

The mule squealed, jerking its head, and moved only when Capo found a cypress burl and whacked him with it lightly.

Swearing, Capo caught the lines and started up the incline toward the knoll. Longarm staggered, leading his saddle horse out of the mud onto dry land.

As he stumbled forward, a rifle cracked twice in rapid succession, blasting the thick silence.

Chapter 8

Longarm hit the ground. His face pressed into the leaves and grass, his clutching fingers dug into the earth. When he stirred, it was to slip his left hand along his body and remove the Colt from its cross-draw holster.

He held his breath. After a moment the stunning shock of an ambush in this wasteland abated, and he tried to think again.

As the rifle shots rolled across the silent swamp, reverberated, echoed, and died, it was as if the swamp itself exploded in mindless panic. A great whirring of wings shattered the tense quiet. Birds screeched and small animals skittered in the underbrush. Just as quickly, the terrified noises ceased, and a new, taut silence stretched across the gloomy fen. The lifeless hot calm of before had become a tense waiting.

Longarm inched the Colt upward in his left fist. He couldn't go on lying here until the bushwhacker got a bead on him. He exhaled heavily. This dark and lonely world was a place of sudden death, but it didn't have to be his. Tilting his head slightly, he saw clumps of fern and palmetto just ahead of him. It was a good place to hide in.

Shifting his gun to his right hand, he put his weight on his knees and elbows, writhing across the ground. From the briars and thickets above him, the rifle fired again. In a split second Longarm flattened his body, felt the stinging wail of bullets inches above his head, heard the fluttering of panic among the swamp creatures.

Lying there, he held his arm out before him and emptied his Colt into the brush from which the rifle fire came. No sound rose from the underbrush. There was only that unearthly silence. The rifle fire and his own gunfire died away. Longarm rolled over, searching the rise above him for the glint of sun on a rifle barrel, for the movement of a leaf or a limb. There was nothing.

The sun braised his face and eyes. Sweat leaked from under his hat and along his forehead, burning his eyelids and nostrils and lips. Mosquitoes and flies buzzed around his face.

He heard Capo moan. The sound shocked him for an instant; he had forgotten all about the guide. That rifle fire had driven everything from his mind. It was part of the terrible spell of this calm and gloomy morass.

Turning his head, he saw the mule standing with its two rear legs in the stagnant water. Capo's saddle horse stood motionless, not even switching its tail at the deerflies.

He didn't see Capo. He felt his grasp tighten on his empty Colt. He saw the shotgun in its saddle scabbard on Capo's horse, and his own Winchester secured upon his own saddle. The weapons might as well be on the moon.

Capo moaned again, and Longarm located the guide. The big man had been knocked down by the impact of a bullet. He had sprawled downslope almost at the rim of the black water. He lay face up, unmoving.

Longarm reloaded his Colt and dragged himself along on his back down to where Capo lay unmoving in the mud.

He writhed through the tufts of grass, the long layering of dead leaves, waiting for the next crack of the rifle. One thing he vowed: if the ambusher didn't get him, he'd fire into the dead center of that crimson rifle fire. This time one of them would die.

There was no shot, only the sickening, waiting silence. Distant, unexplained noises, faint and furtive, merely intensified the eerie calm.

He crouched low beside the wounded guide. Capo managed to twist his face into a taunting smile. "You still here?"

"Where am I going without you?" Longarm whispered.

The halfbreed coughed and blood seeped from his mouth. After a moment he managed to speak. "That's a good . . . question. Right now . . . it's a hell of a good question."

Staring at the hole torn in the mahogany-colored flesh of Capo's stomach, Longarm winced. There was no sense trying to fool himself. This wound was fatal.

Capo was barely moving, breathing raspingly. Blood gorged up into his mouth and he opened his lips to let the dark fluid run along his chin.

"Jesus," Capo whispered. "It hurts like shit . . . Goddammit, jus' when I was . . . makin' . . . two bucks an hour." He coughed helplessly. "Meant to buy Leona . . . new dress . . . with profits. Only the best for Leona . . . that little bitch."

"Take it easy, Capo." Longarm searched the underbrush above them for any sign of movement. He laid the flat of his hand on Capo's shoulder.

"Take . . . easy?" Capo gasped and grimaced. "What for? I ain't goin' nowhere."

"You're a good man, Capo."

"So are . . . you, for a white man." The blood almost choked him and he managed to blow it from his clogged nostrils. "Oh, shit . . . this is a hell of a way to die . . . but I reckon they ain't no good way."

"They're working on one," Longarm whispered, scanning the ridge for any trace of movement. Not even a leaf rustled in the faint breeze.

"Tell Leona . . . not . . . to wait." Capo grimaced with a charge of unbearable agony, blood leaking from the corner of his mouth. His head sagged and for a long, tense moment he was silent.

A death gurgle welled in his throat. Capo choked on his own blood. He tried to cry out and could not. A shudder wracked his body. He sank back, his empty eyes glassy and staring. He was dead.

Longarm crouched over the dead guide, rage building in the pit of his belly. The sun blazed down on his back and glittered in Capo's sightless eyes.

For a moment, Longarm stayed where he was. The persistent waiting silence didn't reassure him. He felt no better that the bushwhacker had not fired again. One thing was for certain. The bastard was hiding out there somewhere, waiting.

Longarm's jaw tightened. Well, damned if he'd play that

profitless game. Whatever he did, he was not going to wait. He'd go looking for death—one way or the other, his or theirs. Right now, it didn't matter a hell of a lot.

He drew the back of his hand across his sweat-blurred eyes. What terror did a stupid backwoods rifleman hold for him in the face of being alone and lost in this wet land?

He glanced around; his own Winchester waited, with the machete tied to the saddle beside it. But he didn't go to his own horse. Instead, he unsheathed the shotgun from Capo's saddle and took the razor-sharp machete from its croker sacking holder.

He dropped extra shotgun shells into his shirt pocket and levered the gun open to be sure it was loaded.

His nerves drawn taut and twisted into knots in his belly, he took a last look around this place, at Capo sprawled dead between the horse and the mule, the motionless black water reflecting dead trees and dead sky.

He searched the ridge above him and then, holding the shotgun in his left fist at his side, he gripped the machete handle and started up the slope. He crouched as low as he could, offering as meager a target as possible.

When he reached the brink of the thickets bearding the dry ridge, Longarm lopped off a foot or so of the brushtop as he moved.

He pushed forward, chopped, and waited, holding his breath. There was no movement, no sound anywhere around him.

He reached out and backhanded the top off a bayberry bush. He wasn't clearing a path for himself; the undergrowth wasn't that thick. He wanted to mark a return trail to his horses and supplies . . . if he needed a way back.

He held his breath and strained, listening for the crackling of bushes, a broken limb, a footstep. There was nothing.

He worked his way directly upward toward the place from which the bushwhacker had fired. He wasn't likely to forget that direction soon. And he had emptied his gun into these dwarf palmettos and ferns and briars.

Though the place was well marked in his mind, it took a long time to find where the skulking ambusher had waited. His eyes fixed on the leaves and mud, he searched the area around the bole of an aged bay gum tree.

The sun glittered on something and winked up at him from

the leaves. Longarm knelt. He picked up an empty rifle-shell casing. It wasn't still hot, but it was new.

"You son of a bitch," Longarm whispered under his breath.

He crouched against the rough tree bole for a moment, his fist closed over that spent casing. He found two others in the leaves.

He located the place where the backshooter had hunkered in behind the bay, a place from which he had an unobstructed if less than perfect view of the horses and the rim of the cypress bog.

The man had left the deep imprint of dug-in bootheels. The heel leather had chewed deeply into the leaves and mud, leaving crescents in the mire.

Whoever the killer was, he must have been watching them cross the cypress swamp. He must have trailed them for a long time, then waited for them on this incline. The marks showed that the man had squatted here on his haunches for a long wait with the terrible patience of a hungry hunter, hunkered the way these squirrel-hunting bastards did.

Longarm searched for heel or boot prints leading away from the bay tree. He found no sign in any direction. It was as if the stalker had moved away like a wraith on the wind, vanished like a shadow in shadows.

Longarm swore under his breath. Even when you were smart enough to know better, you began to believe fearful and fantastic things about this gloomy place.

He felt the hair rise on the nape of his neck.

Slowly searching the undergrowth, Longarm realized he had better and more urgent reasons for a sense of desperation. The killer had moved away from the tree, leaving no trace. But how far had he gone? Was he squatting in deeper brush a few feet away, waiting for a good, clean target?

Longarm crouched low, searching the underbrush. From his early life in West Virginia, he'd brought one hard-learned lesson: No rifleman in country like this wasted ammunition. You hoarded it because your life could depend on it.

Whacking at the bushes, then ducking low, Longarm made his way up the ridge for some yards.

He found nothing, not even a broken twig on the ground to show where a man might recently have passed.

A ten-foot snake slithered out of a palmetto and sidled away, its bloated body undulating obscenely on the wet leaves, unhurried, too aged, experienced, and invulnerable to show fear. Longarm watched the reptile slink into the open trunk of a dead cypress and silently disappear.

Longarm gazed along the crest of the ridge. It seemed to him that a woodsman wouldn't retreat upward, where he might be glimpsed along the sky. He turned and hacked a wide angling path back down to the edge of the black water. Keeping his head down, he went several hundred yards along the silent, stagnant pools.

He found narrow rut marks where a dugout might have been run ashore.

He felt a sense of satisfaction. He hadn't accomplished a damned thing, but he had proved to himself he was not dealing with a wraith or a ghost in this ghostly swamp. The man had come in here silently in a pirogue, and it looked as if he might have left the same way.

He had come in a roundabout half-circle from where he'd left Capo's body and the horses. He knew they lay somewhere to the left of him. He had only to follow the twisting, muddy shoreline.

He didn't want to. He gazed at those dead, black trees, rearing against the sky and reflected in the stagnant water. The purpled haze was like a thin curtain. One almost felt a man could hide in plain sight out there simply by remaining motionless, becoming a part of that dead stillness.

He followed the trail he'd hacked in the underbrush back along the incline, past the bay tree, and down the slope to the horses.

He came down to the animals, a terrible sense of wrong spreading in his empty belly. Something was awry, out of joint. And then it was as if a fist clutched at his belly when he saw what it was.

Capo's body was gone.

Chapter 9

Longarm had the wild feeling that none of this was real, as if he had walked into a wet and eerie nightmare. Crouched low between the pack mule and the saddle horse, he searched the ground where Capo had died. The guide had not been dragged away, either into the black swamp waters or up the incline into the fern and palmetto thickets.

Longarm cursed under his breath. He found no sign, either, that the pirogue had been run ashore here. It was almost as if Capo had simply gone straight up to heaven.

He shook his head, realizing what a perilous position he was in, and for the first time he understood some of what Capo had tried to warn him about.

Longarm stood lost and alone on the rim of a purple-shadowed swamp of dead cypress and black, stagnant water. Somewhere in this morass a killer very likely watched every move he made.

For a long beat, he remained at the edge of the water. Shafts of sunlight glinted in the wet surface and bounced painfully into his eyes. He looked around, not moving, because there was no place to go.

He stared west across the mist-hazed cypress swamp. He wanted to turn back, because nothing else made good sense.

Damn your hide, he thought, *if you had a lick of sense — and knew where in the hell you were—you'd go back to civilization and hire you a more careful cuss of a guide.*

He shook his head. It was one hell of a lot easier said than done. The sun hung like a beacon in the west, but how long would it pause there? And what would he do when the sun dipped below the horizon and he straggled through that black and trackless wet wasteland?

That swamp was one piss-poor place for a man alone to lose himself. Every dead cypress tree looked like every other dead cypress tree. The stagnant water didn't run anywhere; it just rotted there, scum-covered, weed-littered, dead. That meant there was not even a current to follow toward some kind of viable river. There was undoubtedly a river, but he would likely be dead long before he found it, trying to fight his way across that slough.

He stared at the unmarked swamp and shook his head. Then he turned and stared upward toward the crest of the ridge. This bear-, snake-, and panther-infested forest offered his best hope. But he couldn't overlook the fact that one hidden backshooter had already disputed that passage. He couldn't escape the sense that the ambusher was still out there, silent and deadly, watching him.

Longarm had only two choices: turn back across the swamp and face a wet death, wandering in circles in a stagnant, sluggish bog: or go forward into unknown forests where a conscienceless killer waited to stalk him.

One thing was certain. He couldn't stay here. He glanced about the broken, dark marshland, the silent rise of the hammock. He thought about Capo, the way he had been slain, and the way his body simply disappeared into the shadows. Apprehension slithered through him, making the backs of his legs weak.

At that moment a covey of birds took flight from the twisted, shadowy grasslands, and with them went the very last trace of Longarm's irresolution. He was going to move forward. He was going to escape this place, even if he got no further than a bushwhacker's bullet. Damned if they'd pin him down here and kill him off at their convenience. *You're going to do something, old son,* he told himself, *even if it's wrong.*

Now that he'd determined to move, Longarm remembered something Capo had said. Capo had hoped to reach a Thicket settlement called Clayville by dark. Alone, there was little hope that he could find the village before sunset. But he could hold it out in front of him as a goal. Clayville was there somewhere, and he would find it.

He dug back into his mind, trying to remember more of what Capo had said about Clayville. He'd asked if Capo had any idea how far they were from the settlement. Capo had shaken his head. He didn't know how far. "We hit a ridge," Capo had said, "we head left." The trick, Capo had said, was not to look for Clayville, but to seek a river big enough to carry the strange, light riverboats that plied the Big Thicket backwaters. Somewhere, on one of those rivers, Capo had said, there would be settlements. One of them might even be Clayville.

Longarm felt his spirits lift. He was still lost, still haunted by apprehensions that seemed to steam up from the dank earth in this place, still stalked by an unseen killer—but he had a goal.

Once he started thinking his way out of this maze, his mind tossed other bits up into his consciousness for consideration. Smiling faintly, Longarm went to Capo's saddle horse. From the guide's rucksack, he took the handmade map of the Big Thicket Capo had scribbled and sketched with no concern for scale. Hell, he had learned back in Galveston that even detailed survey maps lied about distances in the East Texas forests. This was certainly not intentional falsification; it was just that the trackless masses of water and forest formed uncounted miles in crazy-quilt patchwork.

Capo had made no effort to suggest size, distance, or mileage. These matters had been unimportant. He'd marked the rivers, the swamps, the dry forests, the scrublands, and the few far-apart settlements.

Longarm studied Capo's map for a long time. Then he refolded it and replaced it in the dead guide's rucksack.

With rope, Longarm linked the two horses in single file behind the pack mule. One thing was certain: if he could force the mule to follow, the horses would trail along.

He carried the machete by a leather strap looped around his left wrist. He held the shotgun in the crook of his right arm. He moved upward toward the crest of the dry ridge, going slowly between the tall trees and hacking a way for the animals when he had to.

He climbed steadily, pulling the lines of the mule. When he reached a place where the land crested a knoll, he paused and stood listening. There was no sound behind him. It was as if the world of the Thicket held its breath along with him.

He turned left at a long angle along the ridge, urging the mule after him. The land he walked was high and dry, but only relatively so. Around him, water encroached in gutlike, oxbow lagoons in the flatlands. It looked as if water had backed into these poorly drained areas and died there, weed-clotted, surrounded and strangled by moss-choked oaks, stark skeletal cypresses, cabbage palmettos, ferns, and wild magnolias, all strung together by a thick webbing of dank vines and willows.

He tilted his head, staring between the petrified arms of a drowned cedar, trying to fix some direction from the failing sun. But the sun too was suddenly his enemy; it angled, orange and dulled in the wild-colored sky. There was no way to get his bearings at all in the dead calm of this abandoned land.

He paused often, certain he heard movement in the undergrowth behind him. Troubled, he stood unmoving for long moments, listening for the sound that had alerted him, trying to locate it in the deadness of this shadowed forest. There was only the pall of sick silence with the threat and dread of violent death waiting in it.

As dusk settled in, the first wave of mosquitoes attacked from the dead lagoons. Longarm slapped at a mosquito on his neck. The sound was like a rifle shot in the stillness. Frantic noises of panic fluttered from the brush and as quickly died.

The whole hammock became haunted. He swore he heard the plod of a horse's hooves behind him, but admitted that the sound had to be in his own exhausted and disoriented mind because, when he stopped to listen, he was in a tranquil world of unbroken quiet. He shuddered and kept moving through the trees.

Just before dark he reached an abrupt break in the clotted forest. Ahead of him lay hundreds of acres where every tree had been removed in a clear-cutting lumbering operation. The bared ground had covered itself with brambles, briars, and tall grasses. Small pines were already showing the tips of their heads in the desolated arena.

He felt a faint rise of hope. Capo's map had shown a scarred lumbering area and a river beyond it. There had been no hint of mileage. It was simply as if Capo assured him that the creek was there. All he had to do was find it.

He paused and stared across the savage waste. Beyond it stretched other trackless marshes, strangled with slime, laced with deep black channels to nowhere. He had to cross that pathless desolation and awesome silence if he hoped to stay alive.

Tiredly he watched the sun sink. Darkness settled as he reached the rim of the scarred land. Around him in the darkening morass, he heard the cry of panthers, the snuffling grunt of crocodiles, the frightened cry of birds.

He fed the horses, figuring they sure as hell didn't need water. As darkness deepened, a cacophony of frogs blotted out all other sounds. He decided against a fire, and ate some cold biscuits from his saddlebag.

After eating, he felt a little better, and by the remaining twilight, he hacked four long saplings and half a dozen short ones. He set the longer saplings between stumps and held them steady with grooves hacked from cross pieces. Then he gathered pine limbs and piled them across the structure. At each end, he drove long stakes into the ground.

From the supply bags, removed for the night from the mule's back, he brought mosquito netting and, with elaborate care not to snag the fragile fabric, spread it in a draped tent over the saplings from one stake to the other. By now, the mosquitoes had settled on him until his arms and the backs of his hands were black with them. Their singing was a whining counterpoint to the croaking of the frogs.

He ground-staked the horses and the mule around the net-covered cot. There was plenty of woods grass, the kind that appeared on protected thicket forest floors in the earliest spring while open pastures still lay winter-browned. The animals would be better than watchdogs if any human being or swamp creature approached during the night.

Slapping mosquitoes from his hands and clothing and swinging his arms to dislodge them, Longarm crawled in under the netting. The mosquitoes batted against the fabric, singing in frustration. Longarm removed his Colt from its cross-draw holster and held it ready on his belly.

Frogs, mosquitoes, night birds, and prowling animals put shrill and anxious wailing into the gloom. He sprawled exhausted, agonized in belly, legs, and mind. He didn't know when he finally fell asleep.

The sun fragmented through the netting and wakened him. His body was stiff and sore, but he was astonished that he was still alive. Nothing else seemed to matter. He was still caught in the swamp, but he was alive. He felt so good that he made coffee out of the swamp water, cooking it along with some bacon over a small fire.

Packing to move forward, Longarm felt a fierce kind of elation. He felt as if he had won one battle, if not the war. He had won over the dark night, the deadly swamp, and the threat of the stalking killer.

He led the animals across the cleared land to a shadowed pool where a doe sipped daintily. He let his three animals drink and washed his face in the dark water.

Straightening, Longarm checked his backtrail across the acres of stumps for any sign of life, trace of smoke, or movement. There was only the long, flat stretch of scarred earth.

A channel blocked his way, dark and sullen. The water churned, sluggish, black with silt, with patches of white creek-bottom showing in sunlit scars. Though it was a path that likely led to a river and eventually to the outside, he hesitated. The black, winding stream led into what appeared to be another endless swamp. He shook his head, thinking about the water moccasins, alligators, and the vicious crocodiles that infested these deeper waters. In these bayous lay the only high ground. For no good reason he felt safer on dry hammock land.

He shifted his gaze and found an abandoned logging trail that led off through the bile-green underbrush, already being reclaimed and overgrown by ferns, palmettos, and tall grasses.

He walked warily into the logging trail, testing the muck. He slogged through crusted mud and green slime. He followed the fading trail for a long time, coming at last to a clearing where once logs had been loaded aboard flat-bottomed river-boats. Nothing remained of that operation except the fire-gutted shed and the charred pier support posts. He stared around at the place, long abandoned.

At the east edge of the clearing he found a wagon-rutted lane through overhanging banyans, magnolias, and bays. He followed the wagon road for another hour. The world around him seemed stranger than ever, out of kilter, silences dispelled by noises he could not locate or identify.

The trail made an awkward, twisting turn and Longarm saw it was because it suddenly encountered an arm of a wide, black river. He entered an inlet where the silence deepened oppressively in the unrelenting heat. The water of the inlet lay flat and still, coated with green slime. Moss dripped like choke collars from water oaks massing the banks of the dead lagoon.

Beyond the inlet, he saw the few structures of a settlement. Oddest of all was the single street of the village. It was one short block, from inlet to impassable swamp growth, and it was paved with red Athens paving bricks.

Approaching slowly, his shotgun carried in the crook of his arm, Longarm saw old men who sat unmoving in the humid shade. The village was hotter and more breathless than even the swamp and was overlaid with thick scents of jasmine, oleander, honeysuckle, and other sweet flower scents. The silence stretched unbroken across the town.

A pier was lined with small pirogues and flat-bottoms strung with nets and crab traps.

A forbidding sense of hostility spread outward from the silent village, the green inlet, and the dank bayous. Across the bile-colored lagoon the sluggish waters narrowed into a long neck through a swamp and out into the open river. One could pass on that river and never know about this place at all, a remote anchorage, almost inaccessible in these swamps and bayous except by water.

Four young backwoods women were washing clothes in tubs near the end of the docks. When he glanced toward them, they lowered their chilled gazes, withdrawing, hostile. He watched them a moment—they looked thin, unappetizing, sun-braised, and unhealthy—feeling the hollowness spread in the pit of his stomach.

"What town is this?" he asked.

None of the young women answered. They didn't even look up. They continued rubbing the clothes on the washboards unhurriedly.

He exhaled and forced his voice to remain level. "Is there a place where I could get something to eat?"

When they did not even reply to this, he walked along the pier into the brooding silence of the street. The old men in the shade had stopped talking and sat watching him covertly as he led his parade of animals along the red brick street.

The village was bunched along this oak-shaded street as if retreating from the encroaching swamp. There were less than half a dozen buildings. Most lay vacant, their fronts like empty eyes in that enveloping aura of jasmine and swamp gardenias.

He located the weather-rotted sign of the Red Cajun Saloon. He led the horses toward it and paused beside the leather-slicked hitch rail outside the dark building. Three or four horses, loop-tied under a live oak outside the tavern, stirred.

He secured his animals at the hitch rail and stepped up on the boardwalk, his boots loud in the silence. He gazed at the barroom sourly. The tavern looked decrepit, sodden, mildewed, and dark.

Nothing but thirst and the need to hear human voices, even East Texas twang, impelled him into this filthy bar. He'd been in rundown taverns before, but none had ever seemed as ugly, forsaken, and poverty-stricken as this primitive place.

As he approached the entrance, the batwings were thrown open, squealing and cracking against the door framing. Three men came out, squinting and staring at him in the brazen sunlight. They did not speak but Longarm got the certain sense that they were barring his way.

He peered at them, finding them even less appetizing than the women at the piers. There wasn't enough meat on the three of them to make a good stew. Each of them wore battered, rolled-brimmed straw hats that might once have been white. Blue denim shirts lay open down scrawny chests and worn-out Levi's were stuffed into snakeboots. All three wore holstered handguns.

When he tried to step around them, they shifted on the boardwalk just enough to block his way.

"Isn't this a public bar?" Longarm asked.

They stared at him as if he were the unlikeliest specimen they'd encountered in a month of Sundays and nodded their heads, grinning vacantly.

"Come on in with me," Longarm said, "and I'll buy you a drink."

They glanced at each other and back at him. "You cain't carry no shotgun in thar," one of them said finally.

Longarm shrugged, turned back, and shoved the shotgun into its saddle scabbard. But when he came back up on the boardwalk, they remained impassive, watching him, set against him. He forced himself to smile. "How about that drink?"

One of the men nodded. "All right. But you cain't go in that thar front door."

"Why not?"

The man said coldly, "Because I say you cain't. You want a drink, you'll go in the side door, like any stranger or nigger."

Longarm had by now lost any appetite for a drink or anything else in the company of these backwoodsmen. But, on the other hand, their rules of conduct were no stranger than their town or themselves. He shrugged. "Lead on."

"After you," one of the sun-dried men said. They stepped aside to permit him to go around the side of the mildewed building to an open door.

As he moved around the corner of the building, he realized his mistake. Only the fact that he was exhausted and thirsty had slowed his thinking processes.

He took one more step and wheeled around. But he was already too late. A swift-moving, monkey-like man lunged up at him and hoorawed him against the side of his head with a gun butt.

Longarm staggered. The other two took turns slugging him with the butts of their guns. He struck his knees and plunged out into the mud on his face.

Longarm lay groggy and agonized in the mud, but conscious. They stood over him, their shadows across his prone body. He realized they were already arguing over him, his possessions, and his animals.

He shook his head and turned slowly over in the mud. He saw them staring down at him, their guns fixed on him.

"Get on your feet, mister. Slow and easy."

Longarm pushed himself up. His head throbbed with sharp explosions that threatened to knock him out. He sagged against the unpainted brick wall of the saloon.

"Jus' stand, stranger. Nice and easy." The man standing in front of Longarm was toadlike. His bearded face seemed smeared with inner evil, a built-in kind of cruelty. The man beside him was darker, taller, and leaner. The third man was red-haired, his face glittering with large red freckles.

In one way, the three of them were as one; their eyes were flat and dead and empty.

"Git his gun, Eben," the toadlike man said.

The red-haired man cursed. "You git his damn gun yourself, if you want it, Morel. I don't want his goddamn gun."

"You're jest scairt to get near him, that's all," Morel taunted. "Hell, he makes a move, I'll put a bullet in his gut."

Holding his breath, Eben removed the Colt from Longarm's cross-draw holster. He retreated two steps quickly, his Adam's apple working. "All right. I got his gun, an' I mean to keep it."

"We'll worry about that later," Morel said. "Right now, let's see what else he's got on him."

Morel stepped toward him and Longarm slapped at the gun. Morel yelled, leaping back. The third man struck Longarm across the temple with his gun butt. New agony flared through Longarm's skull. He crumpled to his knees, for the moment helpless.

That moment was what the three wanted. Morel picked up Longarm's snuff-brown Stetson from the mud, removed his own hat, and tried it on. "Fine-looking hat. Reckon I'll keep it. Paper stuffed in the band, it'll fit me fine."

"I want his shirt," Eben said.

Morel ripped the buttons off Longarm's shirt and pulled it down off Longarm's wide shoulders. He flung the garment toward Eben. "Git your maw to sew buttons on it."

Morel found the gold watch, the chain, and the hideout gun. He giggled in a frenzy of delight at these treasures.

Longarm heard the third man say, "Them high-polished cavalry boots—they're mine."

Morel laughed. "Hell, T.W., what you gon' do with boots like them? They're way too big."

"I'll fix 'em so's I can wear 'em. I'll fix 'em. Anyhow, I want 'em, by damn."

"All right, T.W., don't go off'n your rocker. Jes' keep your shirt on."

Abruptly, and without signalling his move, Morel struck Longarm again with his gun butt, and Longarm plunged forward on his face.

In a pool of hot agony, Longarm was barely aware of the three attackers. He felt them loosen his belt and yank downward on his pants. He felt T.W.'s tugging and cursing as he removed Longarm's boots. None of this seemed to matter anymore in the sweated pond of pain where his mind simmered.

Morel laughed. "Might as well take his pants too. He ain't

goin' to be needin' fine-lookin' pants like these where he's a-headed—doubt bayou gators care for the taste of pants anyhow."

They ripped off his trousers. Then Morel laughed. "Well, will you look at the fancy stranger now? He don't look like so much now, do he?"

Longarm struggled up from the suffocating vat of pain, wondering if there was any law in this place, and where in hell it was when men could attack in broad daylight. He realized Morel was looking at his badge. "Well, we got us a real prize here. A extra-fancy U.S. marshal."

"Don't favor havin' no trash with the law," T.W. said. "I say we take his stuff and git out of here."

Morel snarled at T.W. "Stop being stupid. We've jumped him now. We got to git rid of him. We don't want nobody comin' in here askin' questions. An' you be in it jest as deep as Eben an' me, T.W. When the ol' gators git through with him, cain't nobody say if'n he was here in Clayville or not. We don't leave nuthin' on him that say who he is, whar he from. We drags him naked down to the bayou and let the ol' crocs do the rest."

"Leave us git it over with," Eben said.

Morel laughed. "Will you look at this here ol' lawman? Here he lies, naked as the day he was borned and givin' us horses and things. Bring a horse, Eben, and we'll tie him across it and git rid of him."

Dimly Longarm heard the sound of gunfire. A bullet whistled and Morel screamed in terror, his voice fluting to a high falsetto.

"Hold it, Morel," a woman's voice said. "That's far 'nough. You jest stand like you are. I got your breast pocket that time, Morel. Next time I put a bullet between your squinty eyes."

Chapter 10

"Goddammit, Willena!" Morel's voice fluted again, bristling with terror and outrage. "You could of kilt me."

The woman's voice was devoid of compassion or interest. "I could of kilt you if'n I tried, Morel. You know that. You all know that. Now stand back, you vultures, and let me see what you got here."

"We seen him first," Morel protested.

"You don't learn very fast, do you, Morel?" the woman inquired. "Go ahead. You tell me. Where you want my next bullet?"

Slowly, Longarm's mind cleared, the wisps rising like fog off a morning lake. He saw the girl standing between him and the sun, but at first she was blurred and fragmented and only gradually came into focus. Now that the girl was here, the three men retreated slightly, and they lost their arrogance. Holding his breath against the pain battering his skull, Longarm stared up at her.

The girl stood tall against the sun carrying a big rifle in the crook of her left arm and Longarm saw that her gaze was fixed on him as if she'd never seen anything quite like him before. She was several inches taller than the three men, and she was the first beautiful woman he had seen in this mildewed hole beyond hell. She stared at him, not blinking and not looking away. She was dressed much as the men were, in snakeboots, Levi's, and a blue denim shirt open down to her considerable cleavage. She wore no hat. The sun glinted and shimmered in her coppery curls. Her hair was carelessly chopped, cut short in twisted tendrils about her face. Her face was a golden brown, thin, with prominent cheekbones and wide-set dark eyes. She set the rifle against the building wall beside him and he saw that her slender, long hands were deeply tanned, but her nails were broken and her palms roughened. She studied him without looking away for some moments. Then she spoke over her shoulder. "Who is he? What did you find out about him, Morel?"

"Here's his badge, Willena. Goddammit, Willena, you cain't jest walk in here and take over big as life."

"Give me that," she said.

Longarm watched Morel reluctantly surrender Longarm's badge and identification papers. He noticed that the three men regarded her with a grudging respect and some awe. It was plain to see they didn't dare cross her. She was a woman, but unlike any other in their experience.

She took her time examining Longarm's papers. Then she hunkered down and gazed into his face. "You steal these papers?"

"No, they're mine."

"You name Long? Custis Long?"

"That's right. They call me Longarm."

"I'll bet they do," she said in a flat voice, without taking her gaze from his face.

Behind her, the three men laughed and nudged each other.

Eben giggled, his voice sounding faintly breathless with inner excitement. "You reckon to dally with him for a spell, Willena, 'fore we kill him daid?"

She jerked her head up. "This here is a U.S. marshal, Eben. You kill him, you'll have marshals comin' in here burnin' down yore barns."

"I tol' 'em," T.W. said, his voice cracking. "Tol' 'em I didn't want no part of messin' with the law. I tol' 'em."

"You was as anxious for his belongin's as Eben or me," Morel accused him. "An' anyway, no sons of bitchin' marshals had better not come in here a-burnin' my barn. By God, I'll backshoot the lot of them."

"Jesus, Morel, you are stupid," the woman said.

Morel's whiskery mouth clamped tight shut, his eyes squinted almost closed, and his face purpled to his hat brim, but he did not speak.

Willena ignored the three backwoodsmen beside her. She held Longarm's badge and identification as if in them she found long-sought answers. At last she jerked her head toward Morel. "That his shirt?" When Morel nodded, she ordered in a flat, cold voice, "Lay it on the ground. Put in it everything you took from him except his boots and pants. You give them back to him right now."

Reluctantly, the men returned Longarm's pants and cavalry boots. The girl said, "Put them on, Long."

As he dressed, the girl supervised the return of his possessions.

Longarm, still giddy with head pain, pulled on his pants and stuck his feet into the boots, yanking them into position. He stood up and buttoned his fly, then buckled his belt.

Willena watched him in unblinking fascination. Tall as she was, she had to crane her neck to look up at him.

"You're a big 'un, ain't you?" she said in an admiring tone. She smiled faintly and added, "Even dressed." She turned away then, studying the items on his shirt. "Is that all?"

Eben and T.W. nodded. Longarm said, "Reckon it's none of my business, but I had a gold watch and a double-barreled derringer."

The girl stared down at Morel. "Cough 'em up, you slimy little shit," she said.

"Goddammit, Willena," Morel said, "I got a right to somethin'. Damn it, I do. I seen him first. That counts for something."

She just stared at him coldly. At last, Morel placed the small hideout gun and the gold watch and chain on the shirt. Willena didn't even glance toward the watch, but she picked up the little derringer and studied it longingly. "Damn," she said, "that's a neat little gun. You could blow a man's balls off with that, couldn't you?"

"If you wanted to," Longarm said.

"Men are dirty, sneaky little animals," she said. "Always

77

grabbin' at you. I hate a man grabbin' at me. If I had me a little gun like this, Jesus, would I use it . . ."

Willena knotted Longarm's shirt, making a package of his possessions. Then she stood up and held it out to him.

Morel looked as if he might cry in protest. He shook his head, gasping for breath and glancing around frantically. "Goddammit, Willena, what you reckon to do with him?"

Willena ignored Morel. She looked at Longarm's identification papers one more time before she returned them, along with his badge. "You got any book-larnin', Longarm?" she said.

"Some."

She studied him for another moment and then, as if reaching a decision, she nodded her head. She said, "Eben, you git his animals from out front. And mind you, you be damn sure you leave be anything of his'n . . . I find you stole from him, I'll whip you, Eben, sure'n shit."

"What you mean to do with him, Willena?" Morel demanded again, his voice frantic with suppressed rage.

She glanced at Morel as if he were no more than an irritating swamp mosquito that she didn't care enough about to slap. She said, "You're lucky to be alive, Morel. Why don't you jest let it go at that?"

They formed a silent parade through the sun-struck village, Willena walking slightly ahead, with the gun in the crook of her arm, Longarm just behind her, Eben leading Longarm's saddle horses and pack mule and, protesting, Morel and T.W. bringing up the rear.

The shack where Willena lived was a Texas house, the kind called a dog-trot because of the breezeway—wide enough for a dog-trot—between the two sets of rooms. These two sections were united by a long, low connecting roof of cedar shakes. The house was made of rough-milled lumber, woods from the thicket around Clayville. The windows were covered with wooden triangles hanging on leather hinges, which were raised during the day and let down at night against mosquitoes, bad air, and spirits. In one section the family cooked at a stone and clay fireplace. In the other part they slept.

The yard was littered with broken plows, hames, whiffletrees, wagon parts, and wheels with spokes missing. Some hound dogs sprawled in the shade of a chinaberry tree. Beyond the shack, at the edge of the ever-encroaching swamp, were an outhouse, lean-to barn, and corral.

Willena paused at the rim of sunlight under the roof overhang. She said, "You, Eben—you put Mr. Long's supplies and gear in the kitchen. And keep your sticky fingers out'n it. Then you put his animals in the corral . . . for now." T.W. and Morel stood, faces dark and sullen, watching her. She turned and faced them. "You two can stay out here or git on back into town. It's all one with me."

"I mean to git my share," Morel said.

Drawing in a sharp, raging breath, Willena advanced on Morel. He cried out and backed, running toward the shade of the chinaberry tree, disturbing the hounds, who set up a yelping.

T.W. and Eben slapped their legs, laughing at Morel. It was evident that he was physically afraid of Willena, as well as awed and cowed by her in every other way. Longarm figured she was the queen-pin around this settlement because she was bigger, smarter, and maybe meaner than the rest of the ignorant natives.

Morel stood defiantly in the shade of the chinaberry. "I'm staying," he announced. He backed to the trunk of the tree and sat down, leaning against it, his face ashen and rigid.

Willena shrugged, turned her back on him, and forgot him. The screen door in the living quarters of the house opened and a hulking blond man with thick shoulders slouched out to the shadowed overhang. He wore a denim shirt, Levi's, and muddied boots, and there was about him even at ten paces an unpleasant odor of mildewed and dead things. He looked at Longarm and said to Willena, "Where'd you find him?"

Willena said, "Morel and the others jumped him in town."

The blond man stared at Longarm with unblinking faded blue eyes. "I mean to kill him, Willena."

"Wait a minute, Cloyd," she said. "This might be the wrong ol' boy."

"I don't think so." Cloyd spoke in a flat, determined way. "He's one of them, all right."

"I brought him because he might be able to help Bubba, Cloyd," Willena said.

"Cain't nobody help Bubba," Cloyd said in that vacant voice, "'ceptin' God. Bubba is dyin', Willena."

"Maybe this man can get the bullet out of him, Cloyd," Willena said. "Maybe save Bubba's life."

"No. Bubba is dying, Willena. And when he dies I am going to kill this man, like as he kilt Bubba."

Willena drew a deep breath and spoke to the outsized man as if he were hard of hearing. "He don't answer to the description of the men that shot Bubba, Cloyd. None of the men."

"He's wearing a brown Stetson hat," Cloyd said, as if this were all the proof he asked.

"There are hundreds of those hats, Cloyd. His hat don't prove it. Bubba described the men who gunned him."

"Bubba was fevered. He hardly knowed what he was saying." Cloyd shook his head.

Willena swung her arm impatiently. "We'll talk about that later, Cloyd. Right now, let's see if Mr. Long can save Bubba's life. You want him to save Bubba's life, don't you, Cloyd?"

"I want him to stay away from Bubba. If he gits near Bubba again, he'll kill him this time."

Willena exhaled sharply. "Then it won't matter, will it? You mean to kill Mr. Long anyway."

"Yes," Cloyd said. He nodded his head coldly. "I am going to kill him."

Willena turned her back on the big, slow-witted man. "You ever had any experience gettin' bullets out'n people?" she asked Longarm.

He nodded. "Some."

Willena jerked her head toward the house. "Then come and look at Bubba. Like Cloyd says, Bubba is fevered, and he's dying. He will die unless we can get the bullet out."

Longarm followed her through the fly-studded screen door into the dank-smelling bedroom of the dog-trot. The wooden windows were pushed open, admitting the only light, plus flies and odors from the yard. The walls were bare, their studs showing, and all the studs were lined with pegs and ten-penny nails upon which hung smelly clothing. The flooring was hard-packed adobe. Almost at once, Longarm felt fleas attacking his legs around the tops of his boots.

Cloyd followed them and stood slouched just inside the doorway.

A tow-headed youth lay on a cot, burning with fever and whimpering faintly with the pain in his belly. His mattress ticking was filled with Spanish moss. There was no sheet and no case on his pillow.

The boy was naked, his bullet-torn abdomen exposed except

for a black-and-gray spiderweb poultice that had been pressed upon it. "First we better get that filthy poultice off that wound," Longarm said.

From behind him, Cloyd said, "Poultice draws out the poison."

Longarm shrugged. "Maybe, but it ain't poison you need drawn out, it's the bullet. Depends on what's been gutted inside his belly as to what chance he's got. But I can tell you he's got no chance at all with that slug in him."

"I want you to take it out," Willena said.

Longarm nodded. He'd removed bullets before, and he'd had them dug out of his own body on remote trails and forlorn ranges. He knew he had to be as clean as possible, as careful as possible, and to work as quickly as possible without hurrying. He also knew he could kill the boy probing with a knife a hell of a lot easier than he could extract the bullet safely.

"If Bubba dies, I kill you," Cloyd said.

"Well, that's real comforting," Longarm said, facing the stolid youth at the door. "I'll keep that in mind."

His sarcasm was totally lost on the hulking blond man. "Yeah, you think on that."

"We'll need some clean rags," Longarm told Willena. "If there are any. And we ought to have some boiling water and your sharpest knife, white hot."

"Your knife is the sharpest one, Cloyd," Willena said. "Go into the kitchen and start a fire. Heat that black pot full of fresh well water. And stick the knife blade in the hottest part of the fire. Will you do that, Cloyd?"

"Bubba's gonna die," Cloyd said. But after a moment he drew his hunting knife from its belt sheath and began to hone it on a stone as he went out the door and across the breezeway to the kitchen area.

"Bubba is Cloyd's younger brother," Willena said. "His only brother. Only part of the Lindsey family left around here. Rest of the family died in an epidemic. Cloyd dotes on Bubba. Reckon Bubba is about all Cloyd cares about."

"They're not part of your family?"

Willena shook her head. "No. Though most folks 'round these parts are related, all of them as close as second cousins, at least."

Longarm bent over the fevered youth on the cot. With a cloth dipped in a basin of fresh well water, he wiped away the poultice and washed the boy's flat belly as well as he could with lye soap. The youth whimpered faintly, barely conscious.

"He'll likely pass out the minute I touch that bullet hole with the hot knife," Longarm reckoned. "Probably best thing for him. Whether we can wake him up again is something else."

"Poor Bubba. He was dying anyway," Willena said.

Longarm looked at her. "Tell that to Cloyd, not me."

"Cloyd is out of his mind with grief and worry," Willena said. "He and Bubba live in a shack out in the swamp. They were out hunting two days ago when Cloyd said they came upon some strangers. The men didn't ask any questions. They jest opened fire and Bubba was struck. Cloyd said he thought those men were the Blast Haggerty bunch that's hidin' out in the Big Thicket, and that they shoot first before they ask any questions."

Longarm exhaled heavily, glancing at the girl kneeling at the cot beside him. Without asking any questions, he had picked up some relevant answers. Haggerty and his men were in the Thicket still. They had been in the Clayville area, though it was likely that after exchanging gunfire with the Lindsey brothers they had moved deeper into the forests.

He still didn't know who had killed Capo and taken those shots at him in the swamp yesterday, but it could have been one or more of the Haggerty bunch trying to drive them back.

Willena supplied clean sheeting. Cloyd brought a pot of boiling water and the red-hot knife from the kitchen. Longarm didn't want the big, slow-witted backwoodsman standing over him while he worked. He said, "Cloyd, I want you to get on the other side of this cot. You wash your hands with lye soap as clean as you can."

"Why?" Cloyd said.

"Because, damn it, I told you to," Longarm said. "Killing me is for later. We'll discuss that after a while. Right now you are going to hold that wound apart, as gently and easily and steadily as you can. No matter what happens—blood spurting in your face, whatever—you hold it. You hear me?"

Cloyd nodded. He washed his hands obediently and dried them on his pants legs. Longarm decided to ignore it; there wasn't much he could do about the conditions in this filthy room anyhow. The odds against Bubba were enormous.

Longarm told Willena to kneel beside him with clean strips

of the sheeting and to mop up any blood from around the bullet hole as cleanly as she could.

He touched the ragged, purpled tear in Bubba's belly. The youth screamed once and then fainted.

Cloyd shook visibly. "Bubba's daid. You kilt him."

"He's not dead, Cloyd." Willena's voice lashed at the big blond man. "Not yet. He's passed out. He's breathing. See, he's breathing, but he's unconscious, Cloyd. That's good, because now he won't feel Longarm diggin' for the bullet."

Longarm worked steadily, probing carefully. The knife touched the slug. All three of them heard the faint tick as the metals collided. "Now, let me try to get it out," Longarm said between gritted teeth. He was talking to no one—maybe to himself, maybe to God.

Sweat beaded his face and ran into his eyes. He mopped the sweat away with cloths and dropped them to the floor. With a wire hook washed in boiling water, holding the opening apart with the knife blade, he caught the distorted slug.

Holding his breath, pressing firmly but gently with the knife, he drew the misshapen metal toward him. The breath rushed out of him when the flattened bullet came free.

He smiled at Willena. "Looks clean. Don't think it broke up. If it didn't, we got it all."

The girl watched him with a faint smile touching her full-lipped mouth.

Still on his knees, Longarm made a pad of clean cloth and bandaged the wound. The girl smiled again, not taking her eyes from Longarm's face. "I'll make us something to eat," she said.

Across the cot, the hulking blond man squatted on his haunches and stared at them. "Why don't Bubba wake up?"

"I can't tell you for sure that Bubba ever will wake up again," Longarm said.

The pale blue eyes filled with tears and Cloyd's mouth twisted into a set of stubborn defiance.

"Bubba may be sleepin', Cloyd," Willena said. "Even with the bullet out, he'll be very sick. He'll need a lot of sleep."

"What can we do?" Cloyd said.

"There's nothing we can do now," Longarm said. "Except wait. You might pray. You know how to pray, Cloyd?"

Cloyd straightened, his blistered, briar-scratched hands

clutching at the mattress. His faded, empty eyes fixed on Longarm and did not waver. "Maybe you better pray, mister. You got more to pray for."

Longarm swore. "You people really don't cotton to strangers, do you?"

"You came here and killed Bubba," Cloyd said.

Longarm stared at the backwoodsman. Once Cloyd's thought processes, or instincts, or whatever the hell they were, locked in on an idea, the course was irreversible.

Willena's voice lashed out at Cloyd. "This is not the man who shot Bubba, Cloyd. You're wrong."

Cloyd shook his head, scowling. "I'm not wrong, Willena. He's the one. I saw him. With the other one."

Chapter 11

At times Bubba slept soundly, and at others he breathed shallowly and whimpered in his sleep. Cloyd stayed at the side of the cot, unmoving and immovable. He moaned deep inside when Bubba cried out and he glowered at Longarm when Bubba did not move at all.

"He's gonna die. Bubba's gonna die," Cloyd said.

Longarm shrugged. "He was dying anyway."

"You killed him."

Longarm didn't bother to answer. Cloyd was like tamped-down, corked-up, bottled stupidity. Longarm felt sorry for the hulking backwoodsman in his grief, but he was fed up with his threatening glances and animal-like growling.

He walked across the room and pushed open the screen door. Flies swarmed up from it.

Cloyd started. "Where you going?"

Longarm didn't answer. He found his packs and supplies where Eben had stacked them in the breezeway between the two sections of the house. He took a folded mosquito netting from one of the rucksacks and returned to the bedroom.

Cloyd looked up, watching him suspiciously. Longarm tried to ignore the blond man. It was either that or punch him.

Longarm shook out the netting, secured it to small pegs in the exposed two-by-four wall studdings, and draped it over the cot where Bubba lay panting for breath.

Cloyd crouched there watching him silently, glowering. He said, "What you puttin' that stuff over Bubba for?"

Longarm glanced at the beady, deadly blue eyes, fixed on him, squinting. He shrugged. "Tired watching the flies and mosquitoes feast on him."

Cloyd nodded his head and looked up. Longarm thought at last that Cloyd was going to express some appreciation for what he was trying to do. But Cloyd's voice was a flat threat, delivered without emotion. "Want to tell you, mister. Ain't no use you tryin' to run away from me no matter what kind of head start you think to get. You cain't git away from me no way in the Thicket. Bubba and me knows every foot of this land."

Longarm heard voices rising against each other in the sun-braised yard. He went to the screen door. From where he stood he watched Willena talking to Morel, Eben, and T.W. under the chinaberry tree. The lacy limbs of the big umbrella-like tree provided the only shade in the yard.

He saw that Willena was laying down the law, but the men were not accepting it so docilely this time. He pushed open the door and flies clouded up from it. As he stepped outside under the roof overhang, he heard Cloyd lumber to his feet and plod across the bedroom after him.

Longarm ignored Cloyd. He heard the door slam and knew that the big blond man was close behind him, but he watched Willena standing just inside the rim of shade under the chinaberry tree.

"I done tol' you, Morel. I allow we ain't goin' to kill this stranger. We ain't goin' to harm him in no way." She stared at them.

"Goddammit, Willena," Morel whined. "This here Long has got horses and a mule and other stuff we need."

"Then, damn it, you'll just have to get it somewhere else, Morel," Willena told him. "I tol' you, he ain't to be harmed, and I don't chew my cabbage twice."

"You got no right," Morel protested.

"I got every right. This man is tryin' to save little Bubba's life. He's done all he could. We owe him decent treatment for

86

that, and I mean to see he gets it," Willena said.

"You jest want to pleasure yourself with him," Morel cried out. "That there's all you see, Willena."

She moved with panther quickness before Morel could retreat. She slapped the man across his face. The crack of her palm was like a rifle shot against his flesh.

Morel staggered, shaking his head. The girl pursued him. "Don't you never say nothin' like that agin where I can hear you, Jean Morel, or I'll cut your balls off and make you eat 'em."

Morel's eyes brimmed with tears of anger and outrage. He placed the backs of his fingers against the livid mark on his cheek. He said, "You had no right."

"Morel, you're so goddamn stupid," Willena said. "I'd do you a favor to kill you. I've told you—more'n the kindness the stranger done us, he's a lawman—not some local lawman, but a United States marshal. You kill him, even accidental, and you'll be running the rest of your unnatural life."

"I tol' him I didn't want no trashin' with the law," T.W. said. "You're plumb right, Willena. We cain't kill this stranger."

"You're right, T.W.," Willena said. "You're crazy as a coot, but you're smarter than Morel."

T.W. laughed, an odd, fluting sound. "Yeah, Willena. I'm crazy, I ain't dumb."

Willena gazed at T.W. for a moment and Longarm let his own gaze travel with hers. T.W. was delicately balanced between shaky sanity and uncontrollable lunacy. Morel was actually sane, he supposed, but sly, cunning, and with the morals of a weasel. He was driven and possessed and guided totally by his own bodily needs. Eben was little more than a moron, amoral, with no way to tell the difference between right and wrong. He did well to differentiate between warm and cold.

Watching them, Longarm was not too reassured by Willena's drawing a pact from each of them to insure his safety around Clayville.

"You understand me now?" Willena said.

"You jest goin' to let him git away from *us*," Morel accused her. "He goes ploddin' around up river, Mortonville or somewhere, *they* goin' to kill him."

"But we're not," Willena said.

"Damn it, Willena, I jest cain't understand you. The man ain't got no chance in God's world. Why shouldn't we take what we can get?"

Willena cursed him. "All right, Morel. I'm sick tryin' to make you understand. All I can say is if I hear of Mr. Long bein' backshot—or even shot at from the underbrush—I'm comin' to kill you, without even asking you about it."

Morel's face flushed, then went ashen. He almost wept at the unfairness of this. "You cain't do that. Look at Cloyd there. He's the one backshootin' strangers in the swamp, not me."

Willena shrugged. "Well, you better hope Cloyd don't try to harm Mr. Long. He does, it's going to cost you."

"And there's them strangers hidin' out in the swamps," Morel said. "That Haggerty bunch. They the ones likely shot poor ol' Bubba. This here lawman goes lookin' for them, they goin' to kill him sure, on sight."

"Then God help you, Morel," Willena said in that chilled, implacable tone. "Just so you all understand me. You, Cloyd, you understand me?"

Cloyd nodded, but he still glowered at Longarm. Longarm had the strange sense that Cloyd not only didn't understand Willena, he had not even really heard her.

Willena let her gaze trail across their faces one more time. "Then, if you all understand me, you all can come in the kitchen and set down to dinner."

Preparing the midday meal had turned the kitchen area into a humid sweatbox, but neither Willena nor any of the backwoodsmen seemed to notice the stifling heat or the suffocating odors.

The pine and oak fire was burning down in the open hearth under the iron grate upon which Willena had fried catfish, boiled grits, and baked sweet potatoes.

She served the food on a bare pinewood table inhabited by flies which buzzed upward every time anyone moved a hand and disturbed them. She had placed tin plates along the table, at which two benches were moored lengthwise. Cloyd, Morel, T.W., and Eben sat quickly on one bench, making certain they left no room for Longarm to sit beside them. He and Willena sat across the table from the four.

"Thought we'd have us some milk to drink," Willena said. "Got it fresh this morning, but it's soured already. Ain't fit for the dogs. I'll make some sour-milk biscuits for supper. That's about all it's fittin' for now."

"Milk don't keep in this heat," T.W. said. He nodded and repeated it sagely.

Morel reached for the tin platter of catfish, but Willena struck his hand with a cooking spoon. "We got manners in this house, Jean Morel," she said. "We serve our guests first."

"I'm a guest," Morel snarled across the table at her.

"But you ain't a stranger," Willena told him. "Help yourself to some catfish, Mr. Long. Caught 'em on my own lines this morning. They're real tasty."

She put the largest yam on his plate and spooned runny grits beside the fish. "Sorry we ain't got no butter," she apologized. "It's spoiled too."

"It's the heat," T.W. said, nodding his head. "Everything spoils."

The only utensils Willena had placed beside the plates were spoons. There were neither knives nor forks, but Longarm saw it did not matter. The men ate the fish with their hands and held the peeled yams in their fingers. They used their spoons only to scoop up the runny white grits. Silently, Longarm followed suit. A fly fell into his grits. For an instant he hesitated, unable to eat it. Willena saw the insect struggling in the soupy cornmeal. She reached over with her spoon, dipped out the fly, and tossed it over her shoulder toward the hearth.

The afternoon settled in over the swamp, hot and languid and still. For about half an hour after the meal, Morel, T.W., and Eben sprawled on their backs under the chinaberry tree. They belched and rubbed their bellies and talked among themselves, whispering. Then they got up and, without saying anything to Willena or Longarm, drifted back toward the block-long paved street in the center of Clayville.

When Longarm went in to check on Bubba, he saw that Cloyd too had disappeared. "Cloyd's got gator traps and fish lines set out," Willena told him. "He has to check on them every day, whether he's worried about Bubba or not."

"Gets around in a canoe, does he?" Longarm asked. He found himself wondering if Cloyd were really checking traps or if the hulking man were hidden in the swamp, waiting for him to leave.

Willena nodded, answering his question. "He's got a light dugout. He can carry it over dry land." She drew a deep breath and exhaled it. "I hope you will be careful of Cloyd. I know he's grateful for what you've done for Bubba, but once Cloyd gets an idea in his gourd head, dynamite can't get it out."

"Still, I have to keep moving." Longarm walked back out to the dog-trot, where a faint breeze stirred.

"You leavin' now?" Willena sounded upset.

"I came in here looking for Blast Haggerty and his bunch. I had a guide, but somebody killed him yesterday. Maybe I can find somebody to guide me."

"You won't find anybody here in Clayville to guide you," Willena said.

"Why not?"

"The ones you could trust I won't let go with you."

"What? Why not?"

Willena shrugged. "You said it yourself. You're looking for the Haggerty gang. There's been killing back and forth between Haggerty's bunch and our people ever since they came here. From what pore Bubba said when Cloyd brought him in, it was the Haggerty men that exchanged fire with him and Cloyd. I happen to know that at least two of the Haggerty people have been killed."

"That leaves about four of them," Longarm said.

Willena nodded. "They ain't natives to the Thicket, Haggerty and his people. But they know how to creep around and hide. And they've got too big an edge over you. They shoot and they don't ask no questions first. No, they got too much in their favor over you and anybody that tried to guide you through these swamps."

"I pay well."

"You don't pay well enough to get my people killed." She shook her head, her jaw set. "My people won't guide you, Longarm. And if you found a man in town that said he would guide you, why, I can tell you, he'll be like Morel. He'll have one aim in mind—to get you out in the pig tracks and kill you for what you own."

"You make it sound as if you don't think much of my chances."

She stared at him, her eyes open, honest, and compassionate. "Do you? A man alone can get lost in the Thicket and never even be found, 'ceptin' maybe by the gators and the buzzards. You come up on a liquor still, even by accident, and somebody will kill you for it. Or, if Haggerty's men find you before you find them—and that's dead certain the way it would be—you're dead. And if you had a guide with you, he'd be dead too."

"Still, I've got my job."

"You saw what happened to you this morning. Morel would have killed you and thrown your body to the gators if I hadn't come along. And somebody killed your guide yesterday. If you got any sense at all, you'll catch one of them riverboats downstream in the morning and face the facts. You ain't got no other chance of coming out of here alive."

"This town of Mortonville. Any chance Haggerty might hole up around there?"

Willena caught her breath in a sharp gasp, staring at him. "My God, Longarm! Ain't you listened to a word I said? I'm tryin' to save your life for you."

He smiled at her. "And I appreciate it, Willena. I truly do. Only I know what I've got to do. If I went downstream out of the Thicket, I'd only have to come back later. Maybe with two or three other marshals with me, but my chances wouldn't be much better, would they?"

She shook her head. "No better at all. These people hate one stranger. They hate more than one even more fierce."

"But you don't?"

She smiled. "I'm like T.W. I'm crazy, not stupid."

"And you won't help me get to Mortonville?"

She was silent for a long moment. Then she shook her head negatively, sighing. "I wouldn't be doin' you no favor, Longarm. Folks in Mortonville, they live even deeper in the Thicket than we do. That means they see even fewer strangers. And that means they hate strangers even worse than we do. Only strangers they're likely to see in Mortonville is the loggers when they come in every year."

"How far is Mortonville?"

"'Bout five miles as the crow flies. It's longer than that for a man walkin', or rowing a dugout upriver against the current. I've lived out here all my life and I never been to Mortonville but once." She laughed faintly. "Like Paw used to say, I went up to Mortonville oncet, and I looked at it, and I didn't see no good reason in this world for ever goin' back up there. That's how I feel."

Longarm looked around the yard and at the sun blazing like a furnace just over the tops of cypress trees. He stood up from the cane-bottomed straight chair. "Well, if I'm going, I better get started."

She leaped up too, her face ashen. "My God, Longarm, you are damned near as stupid as Morel. Maybe all men are stupid. I don't know. I tol' you. Mortonville is five miles up river. Five miles through the swamp. Only way you could make it to Mortonville before nightfall today was if you had wings and could fly. You ain't got no chance to make it this afternoon by yourself, even if you knowed the way."

"You won't guide me?"

"No. No, I won't. I got no wish to see you shot dead."

"You won't let anybody you trust guide me."

"I've seen enough killin'. I don't need to see any of my folks gettin' killed tryin' to make a few dollars working for a stubborn jackass like you."

"So, it's up to me to make it, the best way I can."

She paced along the shadowed breezeway, moving like a chained cat, going away from him, but always returning, frustrated.

"You got one chance of makin' it," she said. "That is if you had any chance at all—and I reckon you don't—and I know this country. You start out tomorrow mornin' right after dawn and if you're careful and stick to the sign I tell you, you might jest make it to Mortonville alive by dark tomorrow night."

Longarm shrugged and surrendered to Willena's wisdom. He'd spent one night in these swamps and he'd delay doing it again for as long as possible.

The afternoon passed lazily, overwhelmed by that strange and eerie silence of the swamps. Longarm and Willena checked often on Bubba. The youth remained asleep and seemingly in deep pain, barely clinging to life.

Cloyd did not return, though Longarm had the sense that the hulking swamp-runner was not too far away. Longarm could not escape the troubling feeling that he was being constantly watched. *The code of the Thicket,* he thought. *Waiting— waiting to kill or be killed.*

Willena seemed pleased to have Longarm prolong his stay with her in her shack. When he asked if she had chores with which he could help her—chopping wood, milking, or feeding the stock—she shook her head. Cloyd would do the chores when he returned. There was nothing to do until time to start supper.

She sat with him in the breeze-touched dog-trot and asked him about Denver and the other places he'd visited. When he told her about San Francisco she was fascinated, as if hearing about an exotic place on some other planet. For Willena, even Galveston was an exciting, distant resort of glamour and wonder.

She told him how her father had been slain by a backshooter in the Thicket and her mother had died of yellow fever. With her parents dead, her brothers had decided there was nothing to keep them bound to the squalor and ignorance of the East Texas woods. They had gone away downriver. They hoped to find jobs at the loading docks in Galveston. They had tried to get Willena to go with them, but the city seemed too far away, too strange and frightening, and the back country up here was all she knew. She felt at home in this place. She did not want city people laughing at her country ways. She would have been lost outside the Big Thicket.

"That's not true, Willena. You'd get used to it fast. And there's a lot out there to see," Longarm told her. "A lot of excitement, a lot going on."

She nodded, sighing, and smiled faintly at him, a smile that brightened the sun-browned face and glowed in the dark eyes. "Maybe sometime I'll try to go outside." She laughed at herself. "You know, there's a pine tree that grows in such poor sand that hardly anything else can draw life from that earth. Yet that same pine tree would die if you transplanted it, even in rich soil. Sometimes I reckon I'm like that pine."

At six, Willena went into the bare kitchen and with pine kindling, dried sticks, and oak limbs built a fire for supper.

Longarm leaned against the rough clapboard wall on a straight-backed cane-bottomed chair near the door. He watched the girl work, finding her in her own way lovely and appealing. He liked the way she moved, with the fluidity of a female puma, the firm, high-standing breasts, the way she smiled openly when their eyes met. She was direct and honest, whatever else she was.

"Have to get supper fixed and out of the way sort of early in these parts," Willena said. "Firelight, lamps, and candles don't make much light once darkness sets in in the swamp. And we'd have to close the windows against the mosquitoes."

As if he'd received word through some inner clock, Cloyd returned precisely as Willena set the food on the kitchen table. They heard the lumbering man stop in the bedroom. He stood for a long time over his brother. Then he stalked into the kitchen.

"Bubba," Cloyd said in a flat, dead tone, "he's still breathing." It was almost an accusation the way he said it.

Supper was a simple meal of sour-milk biscuits—two or three dozen of them. Cloyd ate them greedily, admitting he was most partial to Miss Willena's sour-milk biscuits. After the meal he filled his rucksack with left-over ones. "I'll eat 'em with a little syrup sweetin' whilst I'm in the swamp tomorrow," he said.

The hot biscuits were served with sorghum or honey along with coffee and long sweetening. There was no fresh cream. They drank their coffee black.

Longarm sat silently watching the country girl and the swamp man drag the biscuits through thick pools of honey and then stuff the dripping round buns into their mouths, chewing lustily and talking around their food.

When Cloyd finished eating, he got up from the bench and belched loudly. He gave Willena a wan smile, glowered in Longarm's direction without really meeting his gaze, then went through the door, letting it slam behind him, and disappeared into the gathering dusk.

Longarm drew slight reassurance from the fact that Cloyd had left. The blond man was still out in the thickets somewhere, stalking, watching, and waiting.

As Willena had warned, darkness flooded in abruptly and spread totally, chopping away all edges and angles and solid substance. In the blinding blackness, it was as if one false step would send you plunging off the edge of the world. Night clouds, loud with calls of frogs, singing of mosquitoes, and distant grunting of alligators in the swamp close behind the shack blotted out the reality around them.

"We got three mattresses in the bedroom," Willena said. "You're welcome to one of them, Longarm."

Longarm was already scratching at flea bites on his legs. He had little desire to be closed in that room with the wooden windows lowered, even with a native beauty like Willena sleeping only a few feet away in the hot dark.

He'd seen a hayloft in the lean-to earlier and asked permission to sleep there.

Willena appeared disappointed, but she shrugged, agreeing. "Night vapors might sicken you," she warned. He told her it was not vapors he feared in this black swamp night.

He carried a lantern, entered the lean-to shed, and climbed a broken-runged ladder to the loft. It was open up here and the night wind raced through. He bunched dry hay and grasses together as much as he could, then suspended one of his mosquito nets from the pegs and rafters.

He crawled in under the sheer fabric, blew out the lantern, and removed his boots. He lay sleepless for a long time, holding his Colt in his fist at his side. He felt tense, as if, like the native swamp creatures, he waited for some evil to befall him. He strained to hear the whisper of Cloyd's moccasined feet on the ground below. His moment with Cloyd was ahead. It was only a matter of when and where.

He had no idea how long he lay in the oppressive darkness. Distantly a gun fired, a man yelled once, and then the silence deepened again. He heard a whisper of sound from inside the lean-to.

Holding his breath, Longarm sat up, his finger ready on the trigger of the Colt. He heard the stealthy rustle as someone climbed the ladder. A head appeared above the floor line. Willena whispered in a muffled, husky tone, "Longarm? Are you awake?"

"I am now." He exhaled heavily. "Why didn't you call to me?"

"I didn't want anyone to know I was here," she said. "And I wasn't sure I wouldn't turn back."

He laughed almost inaudibly. "But now you're sure."

"Yes, it's all right now." Willena came up from the ladder and stood beside the mound of hay where he lay.

Longarm stared up at her in the darkness. She wore only her blue denim shirt, its tails touching at her thighs. When she didn't move, he said, "What do you want?"

"I don't know," she said in a troubled tone. "I know I want something. I have all day. But I don't know what it is. Not for sure."

He held the netting open. "Why don't you come in here with me and we'll try to figure out what it is you want."

"All right." She laughed lightly to conceal her longing. "I know you're going to think I'm plumb awful."

"I hope not," he said.

She laughed at him. "I didn't mean that way. I mean, I know no lady would come up here like this."

"She might," Longarm whispered, "if she really wanted to."

She sank down beside him and exhaled heavily. "I really wanted to," she said. "I lay in my bed down there, but all I could think about was you up here."

He drew her down beside him and kissed her lips gently. He loosened the single button that fastened her blue denim shirt. It fell open and he felt her body quiver in reaction. He closed his hand over the high-standing globe of her breast. He heard her gasp for breath.

"Oh, yes," she whispered. "Oh, I needed your hands on me like that. How I needed your hands to soothe me."

He grinned. "My hands won't soothe you, Willena. They'll drive you crazy."

"Oh, I hope so." She pressed closer to him, but he felt her trembling.

No matter how gentle he was, how patient and careful, she trembled violently. He felt the heat rising from her flesh, the throbbing torment of her body, the aching need that kept her here, but he also knew she was as frightened as a doe.

He kissed her mouth and drew his lips up her cheeks. "Are you a virgin, Willena?" he whispered into her ear.

She caught her breath, hesitated a beat, then shook her head from side to side. "No," she whispered, "I ain't no virgin. I ain't been a virgin since I was ten years old. But I might as well be. I've had it before—sometimes when I wanted it, and sometimes when I didn't. But neither way mattered. I never liked it."

He held her head upon his shoulder, feeling her trembling subside as he caressed her taut nipples, her bulging breasts.

"We don't have to do it, Willena," he said. "You don't have to. You don't owe me anything."

"Owe you has nothing to do with it. It's inside me where I'm all mixed up. You look good. Prettiest man ever I laid eyes on. Good enough 'most to eat. I feel crazy. Like I'd like to get you inside me an' keep you there. Oh, I want you to touch me. I reckon I want it all. I'm all mixed up inside. I don't know what I want."

"Why don't we lie here and you let me love you—gentle like this—and then you tell me what you want."

"I already know what I want," she said. "I want you to do what you want to, whatever it is. If'n I like it, it'll be like a dream come true. If'n I don't—well, I never have liked it. Only before I never have wanted it."

He let her undress him and this pleased and roused her. She kissed his chest and massaged the tendons and muscles furiously. But she remained nervous, like a fish on a line, coming toward him, running away, fighting him, trying to surrender.

At last she placed her bent knees apart and lay naked, panting and waiting for him. He raised himself upon his elbows and looked at her. Her body was golden, even in the dark, slender, with those breasts standing full and firm, her belly flat, her hips supple, her legs long and beautifully molded. He lifted himself above her with her knees on each side of him. Willena came upward to him, at first slowly, as if still uncertain. He slipped his arms under her shoulders and covered her lips with his mouth. She shuddered and thrust herself up to him, whispering his name in wild abandon.

He moved upon her and she held her breath for long moments, flailing her hips, digging her nails into his back. She was driven past sanity, more enthralled than she could ever have dreamed she would be. She trembled, but now it was with desire and anticipation. Her eyes were half-closed, her nostrils flared, her breath hot against his face. She closed her legs and her arms about him fiercely, with a strength that was startling.

He drove himself to her and kissed her parted mouth, feeling the heat of her tongue, the hotness of her face and body, the way she opened herself to him, wider and wider, like a flower unfolding. It was as if she truly wanted to take all of him inside her, as if there were no other way to satisfy the cravings that wracked her mind and body.

It seemed as if the temperature reached the fire-point of a steel furnace under the netting and their bodies fused together with the heat. Her slender arms closed like metal bands about his shoulders, straps that could not be broken. She spoke to him, but in madness, her words making no sense even to her, but creating a fearful urgency in both of them, as her arms and legs closed more tightly upon him.

He had no idea what she was saying, but he knew the words

did not matter. She flared to a wild, keening finish ahead of him, weeping and laughing exultantly as she clung to him, letting him drive himself to her. As he worked, she rose with him again, whimpering and crying out, and then she lay helpless beneath him and neither of them moved for a long time. He felt a shudder go through her and she sagged, spent, into the hay, but her hands still clung to him, her ankles remained locked about him.

The swamp silence and darkness pressed in over them.

Chapter 12

Longarm plodded north on the ill-defined path that followed the river through patches of morning fog. He heard the muffled outcries of animals, a panther's distant plaint, the whoop of cranes. Even the wind stuttering through the high branches of the swamp trees had its own strange way of sighing. The steaming fog deepened the sense of mystery and isolation.

It was the middle of the morning before the sun penetrated far enough into the swamp to burn off the drifting haze. Tall pines stood disembodied, ghost-like in pale gray mists.

He pushed his way through the vapors, the entwined vines, shrubs, palmettos, grasses, and mosses that were tangled and webbed and meshed together by time.

Longarm carried only a small, carefully stowed backpack with enough food to get him to Mortonville, and to sustain him if, as Willena suspected, he got lost a couple of times on the way. He also had a machete, shotgun shells, folded mosquito netting, a clean shirt, and Capo's crude map.

His Colt was in its cross-draw holster and the little derringer was hooked to the chain of the gold watch in his watch pocket. He'd debated between the Winchester and the shotgun; he had decided to carry the 12-gauge.

He thought about the way Willena had awakened this morning, clinging to him. She'd kissed his mouth, his throat, along his chest, and downward. He'd caught her head in his hands. "I've got to get to Mortonville by dusk, remember?"

"I don't want you to go," she had whispered, nuzzling him fiercely. "I never met nobody like you. I thought I didn't even like it. I hated it." She shivered. "Now I don't know what I'll do without it . . . or you."

"You got a long life ahead of you, Willena. You ought to get out of this godforsaken hole. Go to Galveston. Try to find your brothers."

It was as if she hadn't heard him. "I don't want you to go."

He had grinned, feeling his body respond. He had to hit the trail, but his departure had been delayed. He had let her love him, caress and kiss and nurse him, growing frantic, before he drew her down to him.

Afterwards, they had lain together in the brightening daylight. Longarm had said, "You still won't guide me?"

"I don't want you to go."

"You got a one-track mind."

"You'll get killed up in those woods—if not by the swamp people, by Haggerty and his gang. I can't send anyone with you and I can't let you go alone."

He'd placed the small derringer in her hand. "You liked it," he had said. "I want you to have it."

But Willena would not take it. "God knows you're going to need all the protection you can get up in that thicket. If . . . when you come back you can give it to me, if you still want to."

He had lain there in the hay, regaining his strength, and planning what he'd take with him. Willena had been helpful here, at least. She'd told him a horse or a mule would only be impediments on the trail to Mortonville; there was no place to ride.

When he had stowed his backpack, he had given Willena a light kiss. "All this stuff and the horses, saddles, and mules— You can have it if I don't get back this way."

"You've given me enough."

"I haven't given you anything. You saved my life."

"You saved mine too in a way. You showed me what my life could be."

100

"You could sell that stuff. It would help you get to Galveston."

She had clung to him for a moment. "I'd a heap rather have you come back here to me for even one more night than to have all the horses and mules in Texas."

The trail was poorly marked, infrequently traveled, and, in most places, the swamp was trying to reclaim it.

Longarm found it impossible to follow the path quietly. Palmetto fronds reached out, caught at his legs, and crackled as he passed. Vines snagged at him like witches' fingers, quivering and shaking as he broke free, and spraying water from overhanging limbs.

He entered a leaf-padded hammock, dodging between tall, dark trees. It was quieter now and suddenly he heard clearly the sound that had nagged at him for a long time, like a whisper from the direction of the river.

Going taut, Longarm paused between the trees. He held his breath, listening. It seemed to him in that split second that every creature in the thicket hesitated, tense and waiting with him. Cranes and herons took flight from the thick grasses alongside the river, their wings loud in the stunned silence.

He stared toward the river. Either the alligators or some other predator had disturbed the long-legged birds. He could barely see the outline of the stream through the mists laced between the tall, dark trees.

He remained unmoving, listening. He felt sweat marble on his forehead, and a deerfly crawled along his neck, but he stayed frozen.

After a long, eternal moment of waiting he heard that whisper of sound again. That sound did come from the river. He was certain it was the merest touch of a dugout paddle that barely kissed the water.

He pressed against a tree. The sound was repeated, as if someone were forced to work against the current of the black creek.

He told himself that it meant someone was following him upstream. He cursed under his breath because he was certain he could name his pursuer; that stupid, swamp-wise Cloyd.

Longarm padded from tree to tree, going as close to the bank of the stream as possible. The dark waters and tall grasses and overhanging trees were steaming in the mist.

He crouched in the underbrush, scanning the river. He cursed silently. The mist was blurring his vision, blinding him to anything more than a few yards away in the swamp river.

He forced himself to remain down and searched the mist-shrouded waterway, the overhanging limbs, the grass flats.

He sagged against the bole of a tree at last, giving it up; there was no sign of movement in the creek. The mist seemed to smoke across the face of the black water, reflected in it, in a dead and silent world that had not been disturbed since time began.

He got up slowly, slapping mud from the knees of his pants. He looked about. The whole forest looked the same now, trees strung together on thick gray cords of mist. There was no sun to guide him, only the impenetrable, waiting fog.

He found the place where he'd stopped on the faint, winding path. He located a heelmark and set his direction from that.

Glancing once more, hopelessly, but as if impelled, toward the river, he plodded forward along the path.

He had taken less than six steps when he heard noise again. It was faint but certain. Only now it did not come from the river at all. It came from the swamp on the other side of him and the trail.

He stepped against a tree to lose himself as well as possible in the swamp vapors. He stayed there for some moments, but there was only the fragile tranquility, the threatening silence.

Crouching very low, he picked out his path and then moved forward on it from tree to tree. Once more he heard the crackling of a palmetto frond. He stopped dead, sucking in his breath and holding it.

Leaving his backpack to mark the spot, he bent lower and went into the underbrush, working his way back along the trail.

He took a few steps, listened, but heard nothing. The sound was not repeated from the swamp.

He searched for a long time, holding the shotgun ready, his finger on the trigger, waiting for the faintest movement, a noise, a flicker of leaves. He found nothing.

He paused, looking around. He was getting too far from the trail and from the place where he'd left his backpack. He knelt in the damp underbrush and waited. One thing was certain: as swamp-smart as Cloyd Lindsey was, he was still only human, and he could not move totally soundlessly.

His head tilted, Longarm listened. Suddenly he heard the kissing sound of paddle and pirogue slithering reptile-like across the fog-shrouded river.

Staying low, he ran back along the trail, hurrying toward the creek, not trying to be quiet. He reached a tree-veiled embankment over the river and saw the swirl of small eddies around dead logs. He searched the water but found nothing.

He gritted his teeth together. Cloyd was out there, all right. Cloyd was following him.

All right, Cloyd, you stupid son of a bitch, Longarm thought. *You want to chase me into the open where you can kill me, let's play that game. There's no sense trying to hide from you, is there? You know the swamp and I don't. You can keep harrying me until I'm lost, and you can take your time with the kill. One way or the other, then, Cloyd. I can't talk to you. I can't make you listen. But I can keep moving until one of us flushes the other one out into the clear.*

He ran back between the trees, locating the trail and finding his knapsack where he'd left it. He took it up, and socked it into place on his back. Holding the shotgun in his fist, he plodded through the underbrush, no longer trying to be quiet at all.

He went up a small, rounded knoll between the trees, a place where live oaks, bays, and willows grew up out of tall clumps of swamp grass. He crested the knoll, bent slightly forward, hurrying.

A gun exploded from the trees behind him, as if the ambusher had waited for him to reach this elevated place. There was the muffled report and the instantaneous whistle of the bullet scraping past his shoulder like a hornet and burying itself in the bole of a tree inches from him.

Longarm flung himself forward, landing on his knees in the willows and swamp grass along the trail. He clutched the shotgun, waiting. The report of the gun sent up a flurry of echoes and died in the stillness.

That bullet had come too damned close. It had not been a poor shot from that distance, but he had been moving in the mists and, luckily, as he'd ascended the knoll, he'd lowered his body.

Now, shotgun ready, he came up and trotted along the trail, going down into deep thickets of elders and willows near the water.

Crouched against a tree, he reached out with the gun barrel and shook a wet willow. Water dripped as the limbs trembled.

Another shot from the trail behind him showered him with droplets as the bullet cut through the willow bush where he'd disturbed it. This time the gunfire came from closer behind him. The ambusher was running forward, closing in.

Longarm looked around. He couldn't stay here until Cloyd got any kind of a bead on him. Cloyd stayed alive killing squirrels by shooting the small, racing creatures in the head.

Lowering his body, Longarm ducked downward along the cleared path through the thickets toward a growth of cedars and young pines. Once inside this stand of timber, he straightened slightly, running. Another rifle shot whined off the trees behind him.

Longarm felt a trace of security in this thick growth of young trees. If Cloyd kept firing now he'd be firing blind. Longarm wanted to use the concealment of the thick new growth to find a place where he could hole in and search for the backshooter.

He waited, but the ambusher didn't fire again. No country man wasted ammunition. If Cloyd fired, it was to keep him moving, or if he had him in sight.

Distantly, he heard the crackling of underbrush. Cloyd had abandoned stealth now and was running toward him in the swamp.

Using the concealment of the sprouting trees, Longarm ran down the trail, going deeper into the undergrowth.

He ran, but he moved with caution too, making certain that he kept to the trail, poorly marked as it was. All the odds were with Cloyd now. If he let the hulking man force him off the trail, he was lost and dead. Then Cloyd could choose his own time to gun him down.

Running, he glimpsed an odd white brilliance ahead and slowed. It was the abrupt end of the new growth timber. Through the wet branches he saw open swamp ahead.

He slowed, turned, and glanced back through the trees. He could hear Cloyd back there, but could see no trace of him, no waving limbs or disturbed underbrush.

He drew a deep breath, deciding to run for it. Out in the grass and sloughs of the swamp, he would have the same advantages and the same disadvantages as Cloyd—with that one vital and perhaps fatal exception, that this was Cloyd's territory. He knew this region as well as the alligators and the panthers knew it.

Longarm's jaw tightened. He asked only one chance—one clear shot at the backshooting son of a bitch. One shot. He would settle for that. If he made it to the first line of dead cypresses, he might have it.

As he turned back, he tripped on a vine that he saw had been stretched across this path calf-high. In that split second he knew how Cloyd had occupied himself all the previous afternoon.

He stumbled, plunging forward, and heard the savage rush of air. A sapling limb pulled taut across the trail and secured with more twisted vines was jerked free when he tripped on the creeper.

He saw the limb flying toward him in a terrible slow motion. He tried to duck below it, but because he was staggering off balance, he could not do it. He tried to throw his arm up to break some of the terrible force of the projectile, but he couldn't do that, either.

The released limb caught him across the forehead. The world went black. Longarm's head was snapped back on his neck and he dropped, stunned.

Longarm sprawled on his back under the dripping trees. He was not totally unconscious, but only half-aware. For a long time, though he could detect faint sounds, he could see nothing.

He felt as if he were half-awake, unable to move, hot, and wet with sweat. It was like a nightmare in which danger and death approached, but he was unable to react, to run, to fight, or to hide at all. He lay vulnerable and helpless.

Agonized, Longarm willed his limbs to move, but there was no response. He concentrated on trying to force his fingers to open and close, but his hands remained immobile, his fingers stiff and paralyzed.

When he was able to open his eyes, a strange, luminous gold light glittered wetly through the willows. Then a dark shadow crossed between his eyes and the light. He saw the hulking, sun-weathered Cloyd bending over him. He wanted to kill the ambusher, but he couldn't even curse him. He could only lie as if in a trance.

He saw the strange glitter of the sun on metal and realized it was Cloyd's razor-sharp knife. The backwoodsman held it ready to plunge it into Longarm's throat if he moved.

Cloyd stayed poised over him for what seemed hours. Longarm's chest burned. He breathed only shallowly, but he saw that even the stupid Cloyd recognized that he was not dead. He waited for the mindless man to plunge the knife into him. He waited to die, but it did not happen.

He realized that Cloyd was lifting him, hefting him over his shoulder as if he were a croker of dead fish.

Longarm hung there, hoping that Cloyd would bring his belongings. Not that he thought it really mattered. You couldn't take earthly things with you. Still, if there were a way out of this yet, he wanted that shotgun and backpack.

Cloyd's greed won out. He carried his own rifle and Longarm's shotgun and pack. Toting Longarm, he left the trail, going through the underbrush toward the river.

As Longarm's senses returned, he was sourly aware of that dead and obnoxious odor about Cloyd that he'd first noticed at Willena's place. The rotted smell of Cloyd's person was like that of a dog that has rolled in carrion. There was no other way to express it. After a while, Longarm began to feel sickened by it, as if he'd vomit if he didn't get a breath of fresh, clean air.

Cloyd carried Longarm easily. He took long steps, plodding through the mire and underbrush to the creek. Longarm saw the pirogue, pulled up from the water into the sand. He was certain it would leave the same mark he had found in that swamp after Capo had been slain.

Cloyd bent over and put Longarm down in the pirogue. He threw the backpack and gun on the dugout bottom near him.

Longarm remained unmoving as Cloyd half-lifted the bow of the canoe and thrust it out into the stream, taking a running leap into it, landing as lightly as a butterfly on a flower.

They drifted for a long time down the creek, speeding up where the stream converged with the wider river. Longarm still didn't move. The sun was up now, blazing down on the water, burning his face and body like the glow from a blast furnace.

Cloyd sat stiffly, digging the paddle into the water on each side of the pirogue to guide it. It raced along on the swift current.

After an eternity, Cloyd directed the dugout off the mainstream and into a narrow creek clogged with willows, elms, and the overhanging limbs of water oaks, sweet guns, bays, and elders. The sun was blotted out and the silence intensified.

Longarm was thankful for this long journey through the wilds. Gradually, the pain in his skull abated to a dull throb and he was able to think again. His vision cleared and, though he did not move, he could see everything around him. He studied Cloyd's stolid, rigid face, the vacant eyes like open panes in an abandoned house.

They left the narrow creek, coming suddenly into a man-made clearing. Cloyd sent the pirogue racing up onto the bank. The dugout shuddered in the sand and held.

Cloyd stepped out into water up to his knees. He caught the canoe and shifted it farther ashore. Then he removed Longarm's belongings, tossing them carelessly up onto the embankment.

The smell permeating the place was that carrion odor of Cloyd's body, incredibly intensified. Longarm wondered that the blond man could endure the stench, but obviously Cloyd was used to the malodorous smell, if he'd ever noticed.

Cloyd caught Longarm's collar and pulled him bodily from the canoe, dragging him up the steep embankment. On the ground, Longarm glimpsed a single-room shack, an outhouse, and a wide clearing.

Cloyd bent over Longarm, holding the glittering knife ready to plunge it into Longarm's throat if the marshal showed any sign of resistance. Longarm remained motionless, breathing only shallowly.

Cloyd spoke to himself in that stubborn, willful tone of mindless vengeance. "Willena says I cain't kill you. She didn't say you couldn't die. She didn't say how you could die."

The strange, empty face almost smiled. Then the faded blue eyes narrowed. "You die . . . nobody'll ever find a trace of you. Nobody ever know you came near here."

Cloyd held the knife in his left hand. He hefted Longarm up on his shoulder and walked in his strange, gangling lope across the clearing. The smell of death increased, and along with the foul odor came a snuffling and grunting.

Cloyd stopped beside a wet hole filled with water, crawling with alligators, and enclosed in a pine-rail fence.

Longarm gagged. He held his breath—the place seethed, a mud-black corral of the ugly slime-covered monsters.

For a moment Cloyd stood beside the railing staring at the

writing mass of gators, three and four deep, slashing at each other in the mud-hole. And always, rising from that hideous pen, was the smell of rotted death.

Cloyd laughed, a mindless sound. Longarm found it almost unbelievable, yet he knew what the backwoodsman meant to do. Cloyd was going to feed him to his vicious pets. He had the perfect way of getting away with the murder of strangers in the swamp. Once he tossed their bodies into this pen of hungry reptiles, not one trace would remain.

Biting back the sickness that gorged up into his throat, Longarm was certain he knew now what had happened to Capo's body. Cloyd had stolen it and brought it here to feed his stock.

Cloyd was fascinated by the grunting, snarling, stinking reptiles. For a long beat he watched them before he moved to lever Longarm up over the top rail into the pen.

In that time, Longarm managed to free the double-barreled derringer from his pocket and unsnap it from the watch chain. Holding it in his fist, he waited until Cloyd set himself to muscle him over the split railings. *Sorry, Cloyd; I hate to do this, but this has gone far enough.*

Longarm thrust the small gun under Cloyd's ear and pressed the trigger.

Chapter 13

Longarm paddled upstream through the dark swamp in Cloyd's canoe. No one could call his passage easy—the current was swift and unyielding against him, and dozens of promising channels lured him into dead lagoons—but he moved faster than he could have done ashore.

The sun followed him like a blazing eye, glittering from the black surface of the river, burning his skull through his hat and searing his shoulders. Twelve-foot-long alligators slipped from dead logs into the swift running water as he approached, or remained unmoving in the current, their eyes fixed on him and the dugout.

His shoulders ached from his constant battle against the down-flow of the river. He found he made better time by angling across the stream, first to the left and then to the right, going untold miles further, but easing the strain of fighting the swift and swollen course.

It took Longarm most of that day to fight his way upstream to the settlement via water. As rough as it was paddling a pirogue against the currents, he was thankful that he was not slogging through the swamps and underbrush that walled in the narrow black stream.

When he was within a mile of the settlement he could hear voices carrying on the tranquil waterway. He let the sounds of those human shouts and cries lead him off the main course into a large lagoon.

The bayou was like a ladle in the bile green jungle, with the feeder from the river its handle reaching out reluctantly to an alien world. It was strange the way all these settlements had been constructed off the mainstream of this backwater creek, as if the human beings gathered here wanted to hide, to withdraw from the rest of humanity. That each little town was hard to find didn't trouble them. They wanted the isolation, the concealment, the exclusion.

He entered the creek and paddled across the stagnant lagoon warily. He recalled the hostility of his welcome downstream at Clayville; these people had secluded themselves even deeper from human contact.

Remembering Clayville brought the violence at Cloyd's gator pen back in his mind. What had happened to Cloyd Lindsey hadn't been pretty, but it had been immediate. The big blond swamprunner's legs buckled, his arms sagged lifelessly, and Longarm caught himself, teetering for a long beat atop the splintered top railing.

He had left Cloyd where he fell beside the pen. He did not pretend it had not occurred to him to throw Cloyd to his own captured reptiles. But instead, Longarm had walked away. He had returned to the riverbank to reclaim his backpack and shotgun. It occurred to him that Cloyd wasn't going to need this dugout and that a river passage upstream couldn't be as dangerous as plodding through swamps.

Now, he could hear the unusually loud voices of the people of this settlement. He supposed the place was Mortonville; he hoped so. Capo's map showed no other villages in the area, but the way these people hid themselves, one might pass a town nestled on a remote lagoon and never suspect its existence.

Paddling toward the wooden piers where the flatbotton riverboats tied up, Longarm surveyed the town. Mortonville looked even danker and more decayed than Clayville. And this little settlement could not even boast a block-long paved street.

In face, it was as if the lagoon were the main thoroughfare of the anchorage. The unpainted, mildewed buildings hugged the water-line in an arc at the topmost curve of the bayou. Nothing more than a hardpacked footpath separated the stoops and steps of the houses and stores from the open mudflats. Many small flatbottom boats, pirogues, and canoes baked, abandoned in the sun at the water's edge. The swamp hovered over the habitations as if trying to reclaim even this small space from the human beings who intruded upon it.

The failing afternoon sun glittered beyond the highest cypresses and water oaks, laying cross hatchings of shadow across the weather-beaten abodes.

Longarm reached the hardpacked clearing where the other small craft were beached. He had not glimpsed another human being. This gave him no particular sense of security. He was aware that a dozen rifles could be fixed on him at this moment from concealment.

With a deep thrust of his paddle, Longarm sent his boat far up on the sandy shore. He got out of the pirogue and pulled it a few feet higher onto dry land.

He paused, hearing the muttering of voices from beyond the last house in the arc hugging the bayou. Leaving his backpack and shotgun in the bottom of the dugout, he walked toward the noise.

He walked easy, trying to watch the shadows, the windows and airspaces between the shacks. Ahead he saw the village cemetery, enclosed by a wire fence. Within its confines what looked to be the entire population of the anchorage was gathered, about eighty or ninety people.

They wore black and were loosely congregated about a fresh mound of muck, an open grave, and a man holding a Bible. Some of the coffee-dark-faced women were weeping quietly, but many stood immobile, unable to express emotion. The men stood rigid, speaking in unison in some kind of ritual prayer led by the man with the Bible.

Beside the open grave was a pine bier. Near the bier, placed against an empty packing crate, lay the stacked guns and rifles of the mourners. They had come to bury one of their own, But they had come armed.

Longarm walked up the slight incline to the open gate of the burial grounds. He stepped inside the gate but did not approach the gathered mourners.

He was aware that most of them had been watching him covertly since he walked away from the shoreline of the bayou. Their faces were cold, but there was not the hostility he had seen in the chilled countenances back at Clayville. These people

111

might have been just as hostile and antagonistic, but he had caught them in a moment of grief.

He remained unmoving, his hat in his hand, until the prayers ended. Three men and three women sang a hymn badly off-key, most of the words mumbled or swallowed.

Six men remained behind to lower the casket into the damp, water-logged hole. The others turned away. Quietly they took up their rifles and shotguns and, led by the man holding the Bible, they walked toward Longarm.

"Brother," the man said in greeting. He was a rail-thin, gangly man in a black hat, dingy gray shirt, string tie, black suit, and high boots. His eyes were a matching ebony, narrowed and unsmiling. He held his Bible in both hands in front of him and peered at Longarm, waiting.

"My name is Custis Long," Longarm said. "I'm a deputy United States marshal on official business up this way, or I'd never have intruded on you folks at such a sad time, Mr.—"

"Dexter," the Bible-toter said. "Ralph Dexter. I am the spiritual leader here in Mortonville, Mr. Long."

Longarm extended his hand, but Dexter appeared not to notice the friendly gesture. Behind Dexter, Longarm heard whispered voices in the congregation.

"You have indeed come at a sad time, Brother Long," Dexter said. "We are here burying our Brother Walter Slayton. Brother Walter was killed last night, and the town is grieved."

"I'm sorry to hear that. Was he a well-loved man?"

"He was one of us," Ralph Dexter said. "When we lose one of our own, it is as if we lose a part of ourselves."

"Walter was murdered," a man said from behind the preacher. "Don't forget that. Murdered in cold blood."

Longarm said, "Murdered by a stranger, I reckon?"

"In a way they was strangers," the preacher said. "They had been among us for a while. We tried to treat them kindly."

"They come into town a few weeks back," a woman said.

"That's right." Dexter's cold glance silenced the woman. "They did come into our midst as strangers."

"But they was real friendly at first," someone else said.

"Real friendly," another said. "And since one of the Meffert boys was with them—"

"Meffert boy?" Longarm said.

"The Mefferts are one of our oldest and most respected

families here," Ralph Dexter said. "Since they were friends of Albert Meffert, we accepted them."

"I am Albert Meffert's father." A graying, thin man in black stepped from the crowd. "I admit before Gawd, Albert has gone bad. We all knowed that."

"Still, Albert was one of our own," the preacher said, shaking his narrow head. "And since he had joined with these people, we assumed them to be friendly toward us."

"Was the leader a man named Haggerty?" Longarm inquired.

"Blast Haggerty." Old Meffert spoke in fury. "His evil and his gold turned my boy Albert from the way of Gawd. I know it. We all know it. And now we have murder."

"We had trouble last night," Ralph Dexter said. "We have these weekly square dancings. I don't approve, I never have, but we are isolated up here. Our young people—all of our people—do need some getting together. We been having these dances for years with no trouble. A few flare-ups, jealousy, somebody drinks too much moonshine."

"But never no murder," a woman said.

Longarm looked at the people. They were still dazed, disbelieving, numb. This might explain their lack of hostility toward him.

"Never a murder," Ralph Dexter said.

A man stepped from the crowd. "Didn't you say you was a law officer, mister?" The man, slightly stouter than his companions, stared at Longarm closely, eyes narrowed.

"That's right. A deputy United States marshal."

"Then you ought to be mighty interested in what happened here last night. There was gun fighting. We think—we are afraid that Albert Meffert was shot, maybe kilt. We don't know. This man Haggerty and Brother Walter Slayton exchanged gunfire. Brother Walter was hit direct in the chest. He was shootin' at this man Haggerty. Some say it was because he knowed they is a reward for Haggerty—dead or alive. Others say it was because Haggerty had taken Nelle Frailey away from Walter and Walter was crazy jealous. Whatever, this man Haggerty shot him in the chest. Walter's gunfire went wild and struck young Albert Meffert, who was standing near Blast Haggerty."

"Strange are the ways of the Lord," Brother Ralph Dexter intoned.

"So then Haggerty and his men ran?" Longarm prompted.

The stout man panted in outrage. "Oh, it was worse than that. We could see Brother Walter was kilt dead instantly. Albert Meffert crumpled to the floor. Then Haggerty's men all drew their guns and stood the whole town at bay. They took Albert Meffert off with them."

"I can tell you why," Ralph Dexter said. "Albert Meffert is—or was—the only member of Haggerty's bunch who knows the Big Thicket. The only one. It may have been Albert's idea that Haggerty could hide out up here, with Albert to guide him. So Haggerty knew—unless Albert had been accidentally killed—they had to take him along as their guide."

"But that there is only part of it," the stout man said. "When Haggerty and his people ran out in the night, they took Nelle Frailey with them."

"A young girl?" Longarm said. "Why?"

"We reckon for two reasons," the stout man said. "Nelle has been sweet on Blast Haggerty since the day he showed up in these parts. It had been reckoned and accepted that Nelle Frailey was going to wed Brother Walter. They walked out together evenings. They was bespoke. But from the minute Nelle laid eyes on Blast Haggerty, it was like'n as if Brother Walter had never existed in this world. That was one reason Haggerty took Nelle. And the other reason was in case any of us came after them. He said he would kill Nelle if we tried to stop him."

"Also," Ralph Dexter said, "the biggest reason of all for Blast Haggerty taking poor little Nelle Frailey with him is that she, better than most any man up here, knows every creek and bayou in the Big Thicket. If Albert was bad hurt or kilt, Nelle could guide Haggerty and keep him and his bunch from gettin' lost in the swamps."

"So what are you folks planning to do?" Longarm said.

"What can we do?" Ralph Dexter said. "I have counseled my people to wisdom, to peace, to the word of God."

"You mean you've told them not to chase Haggerty?"

"We don't want the Frailey girl killed," Ralph Dexter said.

"A lot worse things than death can happen to a young girl with a band of trash like Haggerty's people," Longarm observed.

"They warned us they would kill her if we came after them," a man said.

"But do you believe that? The preacher here just said it for

114

you. They need Nelle Frailey alive. They need her to guide them in case Albert is dead, or too ill."

The preacher protested quickly. "But can we know that Albert is dead or badly hurt? Can we know that?"

Longarm glanced toward the clergyman. The pastor seemed to protest too vehemently. It sounded great: he was worried about the threat on Nelle Frailey's life; he didn't want any more of his people wounded or slain in an unequal gunfight with professional killers. But he was also advocating letting the wild bunch get away with murder and kidnapping while the towns-people sat idly and did nothing to stop them. And if they refrained, as the minister suggested, what was to become of the girl?

"Don't any of you people here care what happens to Nelle Frailey?" Longarm inquired in a low tone. It seemed less than tactful to suggest that perhaps the preacher had received a generous donation to his ministry from Blast Haggerty. Haggerty would probably be willing to buy the kind of support the church leader could provide.

"We all care what happens to Nelle," a woman said. "We ought to do something, I keep tellin' 'em."

"But we shouldn't go agin the pastor," a man said. He shook his head and spat tobacco. "Preacher Ralph is a lot closer to Gawd than any of the rest of us."

"I don't want the people in my congregation harmed if I can protect them," Dexter said.

"That's very commendable. But I think there is a chance that, if Albert Meffert was struck anywhere above the thighs, that wild bunch needs Nelle's knowledge of the Thicket too much to harm her. I think that the threat to kill her was just that—a threat."

The minister spoke sharply. "If you are right, Mr. Long, and they are not going to harm Nelle, shouldn't we stay out of it and perhaps send our prayers? Prayers that Nelle will find a way to break free from her captors."

"Amen," a few people said.

"They might hurt her and abuse her until she won't be able to return here. And once she gets them to safety, what chance has she?" Longarm met Dexter's gaze steadily, now convinced that Blast Haggerty had bought the preacher's immortal soul for mortal gold. "Once they are out of here, they won't need Nelle any more. Then she becomes just one more living witness against them. And they don't need that at all."

"You're right," the stout man said, and several others murmured in agreement.

"No, no." The minister lifted his arms high above his head, holding the Bible up for all to see. "It is too dangerous, too risky for you people and for Nelle. They will kill her if we try to stop them, I know that."

"How can you know?" Longarm said.

"Because I got to know Blast Haggerty in the days when he hid out in this area. I know what kind of man he is, what kind of animal. I know that human life—even the life of a lovely young girl who adores him—means nothing to him. He is in the Thicket hiding from the law. He will kill anyone who gets in his way, tries to stop him, or betrays him. He told me that, in those very frightening words. I plead with you people not to do anything reckless."

"I'm going after them," Longarm said. "That's why I was sent here."

"We cannot let you endanger the life of Nelle Frailey," the preacher said.

"I won't endanger her any more than I have to. If I can find a guide among you, we'll follow them carefully and quietly. I will try to come up on them quickly and unexpectedly."

"And you take responsibility for the safety of the young girl?" Dexter demanded.

Longarm met the minister's gaze levelly. "I take the same responsibility you do, Reverend Dexter—in doing nothing."

The minister flushed and his gaze fell away. Longarm took this moment to press his point. "Is there any of you who will offer to guide me? I'll pay two dollars an hour for every hour we're out of this town."

"I'll guide ye," old Meffert said. "I know this land most as well as my sons. Most as well as Nelle Frailey. I know the places a gang like Haggerty's would hide out."

Longarm smiled and nodded, thanking him. "How about any of the rest of you? There's a reward for the capture of Haggerty and his gang members, dead or alive."

"You being a U.S. Marshal, you cain't take no reward money, can you?" the stout man said.

"That's right. Whatever reward we might earn will be divided among any of you who care to accompany me."

"God have mercy on you," Ralph Dexter wailed. "God have mercy on you all."

116

Chapter 14

By the middle of the afternoon, Longarm was on the trail again. The sun blazed fiercely through the trees and the heat had them sweating, cursing, and slapping at deerflies in silence. It wasn't easy. Nothing was ever easy in the Thicket.

Getting the five Mortonville men on the trail with him had taken what seemed like a million years, what with his desperate hope of overtaking the Haggerty gang while there was still some sunlight. Moving out was complicated by the indecision of the men who volunteered to accompany Longarm and by the strange obstructiveness of Ralph Dexter. He managed to delay them while appearing to offer every support. Longarm began to build up a healthy dislike for the gaunt gentleman of the cloth.

One thing was clear: Ralph Dexter controlled this backwater village and all the people in it. Religion was like a superstition with them, and they were fearfully superstitious, as the very ignorant often are. He played on their fears of God and God's vengeance, of community ostracism, and of the righteous wrath of Reverend Dexter himself.

"There's not too much sun left," Longarm said half a dozen times. "We ought to use it while we can."

"A fresh start in the morning would give you men a whole day of light," Reverend Dexter said. "I would feel more confident of your safety."

"Waiting for morning would give Haggerty and his people at least another eighteen hours' start," Longarm said. "Finding them will be almost impossible now. Waiting another day will only make a bad situation worse."

"Oh, no. No," old man Meffert said. He shook his head. "We'll start out this afternoon. Hell, me and Ryden and the others, we know this swamp as good by night as by day."

Longarm nodded. By now, old Meffert had admitted that his interest in this sortie was not the reward, or even the rescue, if possible, of the Frailey girl. Meffert knew his son had gone bad, but he could not abandon his own blood. He wanted to find Albert. He wanted to be sure his son was alive. He was willing to endure hardship, face gunmen, and prowl the swamps, just on the slim chance that he could reassure himself that Albert lived.

When finally the five Mortonville men had armed and equipped themselves, ready to depart, Ralph Dexter delayed them all one more time.

None of the people of the anchorage had left the main area of town near the boat docks. They sagged in the thin slivers of shade, gathered under water oaks, sat on boxes or broken chairs, watching silently. When the last straggler of the five arrived, hurrying between the buildings, old Meffert said, "Well, Mr. Long, looks like we can git on that trail now."

"May I send you on your way with a prayer?" Dexter intoned. His voice reached every person in the village, rolled across the lagoon, and reverberated from the dense jungle growth.

Exasperated and frustrated, Longarm had wanted to yell at the implacable preacher to hurry it up. It seemed to him that saving a human life was more important than praying about it. But he also knew that these people had accepted him, at least temporarily; they were cooperating with him. Hell, he had help for the first time, assistance that looked like it could pay off. All he had to do to turn the entire populace against him was to oppose Dexter openly.

The worst part of it was that Ralph Dexter seemed aware of this too.

His voice battering against the mildewed structures and flaring out across the lagoon, Dexter summoned his entire flock to the sunlit area around the boat dock. He stood with his Bible on top of a bait well. "Will all you good people please get on your knees?" he said.

Longarm swore inwardly but, after a moment, joined the congregation, kneeling in the blaze of sunlight.

Dexter's voice droned on into what seemed a knee-numbing eternity. He pleaded with God to hear his prayers. He spoke of the sins of the people of the community and asked forgiveness for them. He spoke of the dangerous mission undertaken by stalwart community members and a stranger. "Help these men on their mission, Lord," Dexter said, lifting his face to the sun. "Help them find the true way. The way of God. The way of peace. Perhaps you can make them see that they must turn back in the face of overwhelming danger. I pray you will protect them from harm."

Longarm wanted to rage out his angry laughter. Dexter had not prayed for the mission, but against it. He hadn't mentioned Nelle Frailey and the slim chance of returning her to safety. He had suggested that maybe God could turn Longarm and the others back where Ralph Dexter had failed.

He got up stiffly from his knees and said to Meffert, "You got a pretty good idea of which way these fellows ran when they left Mortonville?"

Meffert shrugged. "Ain't but a single path leading through the Thicket. Unless they went by boat, they followed that trail. I got me a hound that could track 'em down if we had some piece of clothing that belonged to Haggerty or one of his gang."

Nobody could offer any such article.

Longarm said, "They took Nelle Frailey with them. Maybe if we had a piece of her clothing?"

Old Meffert grinned and slapped his knee. "Say, young feller, that's a good idea. Where they go, they'll take Nelle, and Ol' Buck will trail her right down for us."

Once they got out of town, they moved faster. It was as if Reverend Dexter were a magnet and once they got beyond his field of force they suddenly rushed forward through the Thicket.

Ahead of them, Ol' Buck sniffed out the trail and loped along it, yelping infrequently. Meffert watched his animal, pleasure lighting his graying face.

"Mighty fine animal, that Ol' Buck," he said. "Lot of hounds, you have to keep remindin' them of what they're trailing. They can get throwed off by a skunk or otter or quail or even a rattlesnake. Not Buck. Ol' Buck's got Nelle's scent, and he ain't going to stop till he finds her for us."

They moved swiftly along the narrow pathway through palmettos and huge, wild ferns. Longarm had not thought the backwoodsmen would travel with such speed in this heat, but old man Meffert set the pace, keeping as close as possible behind Ol' Buck. The others strode after him, uncomplaining.

Suddenly, in a thicket of elms and bays, old man Meffert saw something. Longarm, just behind the aging man, saw him hesitate. Longarm didn't glimpse what had troubled the backwoodsman, but whatever it was put Meffert immediately on guard.

Meffert jerked his head around and spoke tautly, just loudly enough to be heard by the last man in the line. "Get down. Fast."

As he spoke, Meffert lunged forward like a youth, landing on his knees and prostrating himself in the underbrush.

Longarm followed his lead instinctively. As he hit the dirt he was aware that the men behind him acted as one, dropping low.

A withering barrage of gunfire erupted from the deeper woods on both sides of the trail. The smoke and savagery of the attack clouded across them.

While the sound was still reverberating, Meffert was on his knees, bringing up his Winchester. "Fire back at them sons of bitches," he whispered. "Fire in an arc. We might wing one of them sneaking bastards."

The five men crouched near Longarm fired their rifles toward the hidden ambushers. Three of them fired from one side of the path, two from the other.

On his knees, Longarm fired both barrels of his shotgun and broke it open, ejecting the spent shells and reloading.

Beside him, old Meffert grinned. "If'n them bastards got good sense, that deer killer is goin' to discourage hell out'n them."

They fired two rounds into the underbrush from which the attack had come. Then they crouched low in the path, waiting.

The next noise they heard was of men scrambling and running away through the underbrush on both sides of the path.

Meffert laughed in contempt. "It's them critters. It's Haggerty's town men, all right. They ain't swamp men for sure.

And I'd bet my boy Albert ain't with 'em. Hell, he'd know better than to let them chomp through the woods like bulls on a rampage."

"Any chance to overtake them?" Longarm said.

Meffert shrugged. "Cain't say. They're stupid about gettin' along and stayin' alive in the swamp. But that Haggerty, he's my idea of a brainy devil. He don't do nothin' he don't plan out plumb in advance. I'd say he's shot his wad here. They was tryin' to discourage us. If'n I hadn't seen them herons takin' flight on both sides of the trail, they plumb would've discouraged us permanent."

They decided that Ryden, the stout man, and two of the others would fan out west of the trail. Longarm, Meffert, and the remaining man would check east of it.

Meffert tied Ol' Buck to a pine stump. He said, "Ten minutes. Go out ten minutes. No more. If they ain't holed in somewhere tryin' to hit us again, Haggerty has cleared 'em out. You find anything, fire twice and we'll come a-running. But after ten minutes, you turn and come back here where Ol' Buck is. We'll meet you here."

Ol' Buck yelped once, mournfully.

Ryden and his men moved stealthily off the path to the west. They were quickly and silently swallowed up by the swamp thickets.

Meffert jerked his head, moving east. The lean backwoodsman followed and Longarm trailed them.

Admiringly, Longarm watched Meffert lead the way through dense underbrush with the stealth and ease of an Indian. The aging man stepped carefully, moved warily and silently between the trees. The sun glittered between the thick canopies of limbs above them.

Meffert would slink through the trees for a few yards and then abruptly stop, listening. Now that the gunfire echoes and the frantic reaction of birds and animals had died away, the afternoon silence intensified.

Longarm sighed. He had learned one more fact about Blast Haggerty. He had never seen the man, but from the physical descriptions—lean, lithe, handsome, and dressed like a Mississippi riverboat gambler—and from information he'd gathered, he began to feel he knew his enemy well. And Meffert admired the outlaw's brilliance even while he hated him. Meffert didn't underestimate the man they pursued.

Abruptly, Meffert stopped in a shadowed glen. He held up his hand and stood, rigid and poised, listening for some moments. Longarm watched him.

At last Meffert shook his head. "They've cleared out on us. If'n we mean to overtake 'em, best bet is to set Ol' Buck on the trail again."

Longarm exhaled. He realized it was precisely ten minutes since they'd left the path. Meffert had measured time by instinct and not by a clock, and his timing was precise.

They approached a clearing late in the afternoon. Old man Meffert whistled once, sharply, and Ol' Buck responded. The dog loped back to Meffert, wagging its tail.

Meffert secured a line around Ol' Buck's neck and held him at close leash. "Don't want Ol' Buck running across that clearing and carryin' our greetings to whoever is in that shack."

"You think it's likely Haggerty?" Ryden said.

"Likely." Meffert spoke in a hoarse whisper. "Buck led us here, and he ain't often wrong."

The dog whined as if he understood Meffert's praise.

Meffert glanced toward Longarm. "This here is the ol' Longley shack. Longley and his woman lived out here until they both died of the epizootic. I figured this might be the place where Haggerty holed in. My boy Albert, he used to hang around this place a lot when he was growin'. Run away from home all the time, and I allus knew where to find him. I'd give Albert two or three days to git good and hungry, then I'd come lookin' for him."

They crept cautiously to the rim of the ever-contracting clearing. The Big Thicket was greedily reclaiming the land Longley had put to the plow long ago. The entire clearing was ringed by tall trees and thick underbrush. The clearing itself was overgrown with wire grass and fennel and new growth of pines in the open places.

The shack, what remained of a barn, and a sagging outhouse sat perhaps a hundred feet from the encroaching forest. The hut looked like a one-room clapboard, its cypress roofing blown away in places, the panes of its windows broken out.

A faint trail of smoke rose from the stone chimney.

"Looks like somebody's in there," Ryden said. By now Longarm had learned that the stout man was the peace officer of Mortonville, never elected or even so designated, simply accepted by his neighbors as the law. Ryden had the smell of reward money in his nostrils and his breathing was rapid. He nodded. "Looks like we've run 'em down."

"Either that or they want us to think we have," old Meffert said. "They could be hidin' in these woods waitin' for us to show in the clearing. It's the kind of trick my boy Albert would think up—and, from what I've seen of this here Blast Haggerty, it's the plan he'd take to."

For some moments they silently watched the cabin in the clearing. Faint smoke trailed upward from the chimney. Otherwise there was no movement around the hut at all.

"We've got to get closer," Longarm said.

"I think the minute we step into the open they mean to blast us to kingdom come," Meffert protested.

"Well, we've come this far," Longarm whispered. "We've got to be smarter than this. We can't just stay pinned down here."

"You got a better idea?" Meffert inquired.

"I've got something I want to try," Longarm said. "The north side of the shack, where the chimney is, is the only blind side of the house. I think I could get all the way to it."

"Unless they start shootin' the minute you show your carcass in that clearing."

"That's a chance I've got to take," Longarm said. "I want you fellows to stay hidden here. You're as safe here as I reckon any of us are going to be out here. But there's one thing you can do for me. Spread out as much as you can. Lie ready with your guns. The minute anybody opens fire on me, be ready to cover me with your own guns."

Old man Meffert thought for a moment. Then he nodded and smiled faintly. "It might work. You're a good man, Long, for an outsider."

Longarm grinned. "Just keep your guns ready."

He moved away from the Mortonville men, carrying his shotgun in his fist at his side. He moved stealthily, warily, through the underbrush. He stepped carefully, watched where he was going. Between every step, he checked the undergrowth around him for any trace of movement. It took a long time to work his way around to the north side of the clearing.

He stayed for some silent moments in the last concealment

123

outside the overgrown clearing. There were no sounds rising from that cabin. It was as though the men in there—if they were in there—held their breath, waiting.

He crouched low on his hands and knees and crawled out of the thicket into the tall grass of the clearing. He placed his gun out ahead of him and then crept to it in the grass. Then he would lie still a moment, holding his breath.

The last slanting rays of the sun above the swamp trees glittered in the grass and burned the least breath of air out of it.

Longarm crawled all the way to the stone base of the chimney. He pressed against it, waiting. Nothing changed. There was only the eternal, taut-stretched silence inside the shack and across the Big Thicket.

For an instant he watched a hawk sail on an updraft high over the clearing. Then, holding his gun in front of him, he worked his way along the side of the shack to the front corner.

He checked along the rim of the clearing. There was no movement, no sign of the Mortonville men nor of Haggerty's ambushers.

Crouched low, he moved along the house, going under the window to the closed door.

He drew a deep breath and held it. There was no longer any reason to wait, no sense in trying to hide. Anyone outside the clearing could see him. If the people inside the hut weren't yet aware of his presence, they would be momentarily.

He levered himself up against the door framing opposite the latch. He cocked both triggers on the double-barreled 12-gauge, then he kicked the door in.

He lunged into the doorway, standing with the gun ready to fire.

He stopped, shocked. The room was empty. The fire was made of damp wood and damp grasses, just enough warmth to send up a tail of smoke through the chimney, just enough to lure the pursuers in here—to an abandoned cabin.

It was clear that someone had been here recently, though. There were no chairs or beds in the room. There was an unpainted pinewood table littered with bones and discarded bits of food. In a corner beyond the fireplace was an old steamer trunk which looked like something the Longleys might have owned twenty years past.

Longarm stepped through the door to the stoop and waved his arm, signalling the other men to join him.

They came in cautiously, three walking forward, guns held at the ready, the other two backing in, watching for any movement in the thickets.

"They foxed us," old man Meffert said. He held the hound on a tight leash. "First they tried to scare us off. Then they moved on from here, making sure we would waste time trying to pin them down."

Ol' Buck whined and strained at the rope.

"Smell of the Frailey girl," Meffert said. "It's still fresh and strong in here. See how Ol' Buck carries on?"

Meffert tried to soothe the hound, but the animal twisted and yanked at the rope in a way even its owner had never seen before. "Damn," Meffert said, "something's got Ol' Buck purely upset."

Watching the dog, Longarm said, "Why don't you let him go? See what he does?"

Meffert smiled and nodded. "Likely, Ol' Buck will take off acrosst the clearing, leading us out of here, but that's all right."

He bent down and loosened the noose, slipping the line over the hound's floppy ears. "What's the matter, Buck?" he said. "What's wrong, boy?"

The dog leaped away, yelping and barking. He ran to the steamer trunk in the corner.

Longarm and Meffert reached the trunk at the same instant. "I'll hold my gun ready," Meffert said. "You throw back the top and open her up."

Longarm nodded. The other men closed around in a semi-circle behind Meffert. The aging man fixed his rifle on the chest.

Longarm caught the top and threw it back. His eyes widened and his mouth sagged open.

A young girl, trussed up and gagged, as naked as the moment she'd been born, was stuffed down into the chest.

"Nelle," Ryden whispered. He shook his head. "Nelle Frailey."

Except that her slender face was twisted in rage and her mouth constricted by the gag, the girl was lovely. She looked to be in her late teens. Her sun-darkened body had been molded with loving care and looked very intriguing.

Dark hair spilled down over her shoulders almost to her high-standing breasts. Her waist was narrow, her belly flat, her thighs and legs shapely.

For a long beat no one moved in that cabin. Nelle Frailey glared up at them and the men, young and old, stared at her in admiration and awe.

One of the men whispered, "Hot damn." And Longarm didn't blame him. It was evident that, though the fellow had been born in Mortonville and grown up there, as Nelle Frailey had, he had not encountered such loveliness before in his deprived existence.

Longarm admitted he too found her exciting-looking, even in her distress. Though she was slender, that body was ample and well-endowed. At last he was able to bend over and, being careful not to grasp anything too personal, lift her from the trunk.

Chapter 15

The entire population of Mortonville came hurrying down to dockside to meet Longarm and the search party when they returned early in the night with Nelle Frailey in tow.

"Praise God!" Ralph Dexter shouted. He shook the Bible above his head in a gesture of triumph. "God has returned our daughter to us."

"Amen." The word came from all the people as if from one.

The minister turned aside and spoke to old man Meffert in a guarded tone. "And those villains, Brother Meffert? What of them? Were you able to capture them?"

Meffert shook his head. "They got away clean. And I reckon Albert with them. Found no sign of my son."

Nelle Frailey spoke for one of the few times since they had taken her naked from the steamer trunk. "Albert was carrying a gun wound. Blast cut the bullet out. Albert looked pretty weak and gray, but they figured you all were chasing them to get me back, and Albert said he could lead them. So they went away and left me in the Longley shack."

Longarm smiled faintly. Nelle said nothing about her condition when they found her, or that, except for the hound dog, they might have missed her. She was a girl with fierce, unyielding pride, that was clear. And she seethed with inner rage. After she reported on Albert she fell silent and they could not get her to speak.

The moment of return turned into a town celebration. Torches were lighted and they brightened the strange, heavy swamp night, and reflections writhed on the flat surface of the lagoon. The people congratulated each other, slapping neighbors on the back and shouting out their pride in their five trackers, the stranger, and Ol' Buck. Old man Meffert could not praise his hound too highly. To any who would listen he poured out his satisfaction. Not once had Buck gotten off the trail, followed a false scent, or lost the traces of the girl. "And we found her," Meffert chortled. "By the Lord, we found her alive and we brung her back."

Only Nelle Frailey remained inwardly raging, silent, and withdrawn during this wild festivity of thanksgiving.

Longarm watched her covertly. She was a lovely young girl, but it was clear that she was emotionally intense; whatever she gave her heart or mind to completely dominated her. Her lovely, dark face remained set and unsmiling. People caught her to them and welcomed her back among the living. They had given her up for dead or lost and now she was home. She nodded and thanked them, but she did not smile.

One girl, not as pretty as Nelle, but about her same age, embraced Nelle and said, "Oh, Nelle, thank God you're back home and safe."

Nelle nodded, her expression flat, her features sharp. She did not smile.

The girl retreated a step, and the underlying enmity between the two belles of Mortonville surfaced. She said in a cold, angered tone, "Well, don't blame us because your fine lover ran off and left you, Nelle Frailey. Just thank God you got home alive."

"Shut your mouth, Mary Hester," Nelle said between gritted teeth.

Mary jerked her head and laughed. She spoke in a loud, scathing tone. "Well, I reckon Nelle Frailey has found out just what that handsome Blast Haggerty really thought of her—"

"Oh, go back home and finish fucking your bird dog," Nelle said.

A gasp of shock burned through the citizens, a surprised intake of breath led by the Reverend Ralph Dexter himself. He stood staring at Nelle as if he did not believe what he had heard. Mary Hester wailed, heeled around, and ran through the crowd, sobbing.

When she was gone, silence came over the revelers. The shared cup of happinesss had been shattered, and no one knew quite how to repair or refill it.

Longarm grinned to himself. It was clear that not even the people of Mortonville really knew their daughter Nelle Frailey and what went on behind her deep black eyes.

Nelle's outburst just about finished off the festivities. Longarm smiled to himself. It was just as well. Who could top Nelle's contribution for the evening?

He shook his head. The prodigal daughter was back home in Mortonville, but in body only. None of these unimaginative people would ever be able to guess where she was in her battered dreams.

The townspeople slowly drifted away. Old man Meffert clapped Longarm on the back. "I insist that you come home and spend the night at our place, Mr. Long—"

"Mefferts have got the nicest house in town," somebody said.

"You can sleep in Albert's old bed on the screened-in porch," Meffert said.

Longarm thanked him, but said, "You don't plan to take up the trail and Haggerty—and your son—again?"

Meffert shook his head. "Not likely. Nelle Frailey told me what I wanted to know. My son Albert is alive. I reckon he ain't never coming back to live here in Mortonville in the kind of peaceful life his maw and I wanted for him. The boy has gone bad. Plumb bad. He's set his way of life, runnin' with thugs like Haggerty. I couldn't never git him to come back home with me. Hardly expected that I could, but I jest had to know he was alive."

"That is thankful news," Reverend Dexter said. "And I thank God you all came home safely and did not pursue those evil men any further."

Longarm stared at the minister. The look in the gaunt man's face was almost an expression of triumph. One would have believed that Reverend Dexter had won some sort of victory here.

Longarm said, "But I can't stop. I must follow those men."

"Then you will have to do it alone," the minister intoned.

"I don't want you to think we aren't grateful to you for returning Nelle. We are. But we are satisfied, and it ends here."

Longarm jerked his gaze around, staring at the other men who had tracked Nelle with him and Meffert. He expected no support or cooperation from Dexter. The preacher had long ago revealed where his sympathies lay, whether he was smart enough to realize it or not.

"You won't guide me?" Longarm said to Meffert.

The aging man shook his head. "My heart wouldn't be in it no more, Mr. Long. I'm sorry."

"How about you, Ryden?" Longarm faced the stout law officer. "What about the reward?"

"I'm sorry, Mr. Long. If'n we had run Haggerty and his men down today, forced them into a gun-battle, I think we could have brought 'em back, toes up. But they got a start on us now. I don't think we'd get no reward. What we'd get would be bullets in the head."

Each of the other men who had accompanied him nodded, agreeing with the stout Ryden. "I'm sorry," one of the men said. "That ambush they set for us . . . if'n old man Meffert hadn't been so spry-eyed, we'd all be buzzard meat now. I don't believe in testing the Lord's patience too often."

"Amen," said Reverend Dexter.

Longarm looked around at the apathetic faces in the torch-light. "I'll pay five dollars an hour."

"Five dollars won't buy you much when you're dead," somebody said.

"I tell you the truth, Mr. Long. I think Blast Haggerty is too smart for you. An' he's got Albert Meffert to guide him in this swamp. You're askin' to die to go chasin' after him." Ryden shook his head regretfully.

"Blast Haggerty is clever. He's dangerous," Meffert said. "We all know him that well. You ought to give it up, Mr. Long. For your own safety."

"That's right," another man said. "Ain't nobody in this swamp country smart enough to run Blast Haggerty down."

"Not an' stay alive," another man agreed.

Nelle Frailey stepped forward. Her black eyes met Long-arm's evenly. She said, "I'll guide you." Her laughter was cold and dead. "I'll take you right to him. What happens to you then ain't none of my affair."

Longarm grinned down at her. "That's fair enough."

* * *

By daybreak, Longarm and Nelle were on the twisting trail through the Thicket, headed north. The first crimson sprays of sunlight illumined the swamp country, lighting the tufts of tall trees and sparkling on mist-damp leaves.

Nelle carried her own backpack. She also carried a gun, a small-gauge hunting rifle that she hefted easily in her left hand. She wore a straw bonnet with its floppy brim shading her face and almost concealing her eyes. It was as if it were her eyes she wanted to protect from the probing of strangers.

She wore her denim shirt buttoned at the wrists and at the throat, since mosquitoes still whined in thick clouds about them when they bumped into the elders or blackberry bushes beside the trail. Her Levi's were a snug fit across her shapely hips and along her slender thighs and calves. She wore snakeboots.

Nelle had arrived at the screen door of Meffert's house an hour before dawn. Longarm lay awake on the goose-down mattress of the cot. When Nelle rapped on the door once, Longarm said, "I'm awake. I'll be right with you."

"You sound surprised to see me," she said, remaining on the other side of the screen.

"I thought you might change your mind."

"I'm not that kind of girl, mister. When I make up my mind to do something, I do it. When I give my word, I keep it."

He laughed softly. "You're one hell of a woman, all right."

"And you can just forget that part of it right now," Nelle Frailey told him.

"Right." He laughed. "All business."

"You try to make anything else out of it, mister, and you'll wake up to find yourself shifting for yourself in the middle of the Thicket."

He let himself out of the door, joining her in the last faint chill of the night. Tints of gray already appeared along the distant eastern horizon.

"I came early," Nelle said, "so's we could be shed of this damned town before these narrow-minded asses wake up. They won't approve of me going off in the swamp alone with you." She laughed coldly. "Not that it's any of their stupid business."

"I still say you're one hell of a woman. I'll bet this town never has approved of the things you did."

"It's none of their business," she repeated.

"Was Mary Hester kind of sweet on Brother Walter Slayton?" Longarm inquired as they strode past the last shack of the village and entered the thick forest that bearded the clearing.

Nelle jerked her head around. "Why?"

Longarm shrugged. "I don't know. I seemed to get the idea there wasn't much love lost between you two. I was just trying to find a reason."

"Why don't we stick to finding Blast Haggerty?" she said.

"Any way you want it, Miss Frailey." He laughed. "I was just trying to make conversation. I don't have to do that, either."

"That's right, you don't."

They walked for some time in silence. At last Nelle said, "All you've got to do is keep your eyes open. I'd like to find Blast Haggerty before he finds us. I think we'd live longer that way."

"You think we'll find Haggerty?"

She shrugged. "We will if he's still here in the Thicket country."

"Even with Albert Meffert guiding him?"

"Albert is stupid," she said. "Nobody could possibly love Albert but his old man and old Mrs. Meffert. One thing I can say without false pride, Long. You got a hell of a lot better guide than Haggerty has."

"Glad to hear it. And I promise to keep my eyes open. You just find Haggerty for me and I'll do the rest."

She glanced over her shoulder at him, her face set. "You're a big one. Look like you know what you're doing. But whether you last up against Blast Haggerty is entirely different."

"You just find Blast for me," he said. "What happens then doesn't have to concern you, does it?"

"That's right." She nodded. "Oh, I'll find him. Maybe you think I won't, but I guarantee you I will."

"Why are you so sure?"

She was silent for a long beat. Then she said in a flat, low voice, "Because I want to find him."

Longarm grinned. "Still wild for him, are you? No matter what he did to you?"

"Ain't none of your fuckin' business is it?" she said.

He laughed. "Reckon not. I can say one thing, though. Old Mary Hester and I sure can rile you up fast, can't we?"

"Just keep walking," Nelle Frailey said over her shoulder.

In much better time than they'd covered the distance the afternoon before, Longarm and Nelle strode past the old Longley shack. The front door stood open and the broken windows gaped. Nelle didn't even glance toward the hut where she'd been so miserably humiliated.

"They're not there," she said, as if answering his unspoken question. "We don't have to check it. They're long gone."

"Did you hear them say where they were headed?" Longarm asked.

"Don't have to. They want to get to some place like Beaumont where they can hire a way to safety. Haggerty said something about going East to hide out, that no law man would ever think of looking for Western bank robbers in Atlanta."

"Makes sense," Longarm said. "I never thought of that idea."

"Nobody else has," Nelle said. "Haggerty stays a few jumps ahead of everybody else. He's got a sharp mind."

Longarm laughed sympathetically. "And a little country gal he left behind that's purely crazy about him."

She paused suddenly in the trail and spun around so that he almost charged into her before he could slow down. Her right hand on her hip, Nelle peered up at him. "All right. You want to hear me say it? Will that shut you up about it? I was mad crazy about Blast. I never met nobody like him in this world. I reckon I never will again. Is that what you want to hear? Will you shut up about it now?"

Longarm sighed, smiling. "I think I have a right to know just how you feel about ol' Blast, honey. After all, if we do find him, my life might depend on how you really feel about him."

A couple of hours into the dank forest they walked into almost impenetrable swarms of mosquitoes. The insects flew into their eyes, mouths, nostrils, and clothing.

"Blind mosquitoes," Nelle said. "They don't bite so much, but they can drive you crazy."

"Good Lord. Isn't there anything that will keep them off?"

"We'll get away from them in an hour or so," Nelle said. "Meantime, I brought along a couple of little bottles of stuff that might help."

She paused beside the bole of a wild magnolia, slipped the pack off her back, and opened it. The first thing she pulled out was a neatly folded cotton party dress. It was the only feminine article in her gear and, as far as he could see, totally useless out here.

"A party dress?" He waved his arms at the swarming mosquitoes. "You planning to dance with me?"

She stared up at him coldly. "I'm plannin' nothing with you, mister, but gettin' you to Blast Haggerty, and likely seein' you killed for the trouble." She gripped the dress fiercely in her fist and shoved it down into the backpack. "I carry it to remind me, that's all." She refused to say any more about it. She handed him a small blue bottle that smelled rotten before he touched it. She laughed at him. "Go on and take it," she said. "It's a damn good mosquito repellent."

"No wonder. What is it?"

"That there bottle is alligator grease," she said. "Once that stuff spoils it keeps mosquitoes away like magic."

"My God. But if you got the stuff on you, could you ever get it off?"

"You didn't ask about that. You said you wanted a mosquito repellent. That's the best. And I reckon the stink will wear off in time." She handed him a second bottle. "This here is rancid fish oil. I guarantee you, you rub that on your neck and hands and you'll walk through these swarms untouched."

Longarm applied the grease gingerly. Nelle watched him, almost smiling. "You lived long down here in the Thicket, you'd get accustomed to stinks. You wouldn't even notice."

"Except stinks like Mary Hester. You don't get used to them."

She glared up at him. "You don't let up, do you?"

"I like you, Nelle. That's why I tease you. Hell, if I didn't think you were special, I wouldn't say a damned word to you."

"Well, just save your breath. I like the quiet better." She took the bottles, rubbed dabs of the grease like beauty cream on her hands, throat, and behind her ears. Then she replaced the bottles, closed the sack, and took it up again. "You know the best cure for the sting of mosquitoes?"

"No. What?"

"Urine. Mosquito bites you, you put urine on it and the sting disappears instantly. Just like stinging nettles. Nothing better for stinging nettles than a palm full of pee."

Longarm swung his arms at the black clouding of insects. "That sounds great. But what will we do if we run out of pee?"

She laughed, striding off down the path. "As long as the mosquitoes bite you, mister, you'll pee."

Longarm watched the shapely, slender little form walking away from him in the underbrush. He grinned faintly. She really looked as if she carried dynamite in those Levi's, as if she were made of wild excitement, whether she knew it or not.

He sighed. Nelle had warned him there could be nothing between them but business—the business of finding Blast Haggerty. She had been badly hurt, and very recently. She not only wasn't receptive to lovemaking, she was sick of the very idea of love. There was no room in her now except for pain and bitterness.

He warned himself to put her shapely hips and high-standing young breasts from his mind. A man stayed alive in this dark jungle world—if at all—by remaining alert to a thousand hidden perils.

He heard Nelle's sharp intake of breath. Instantly wary, he tightened his fist on the shotgun and paused, checking the underbrush narrowly.

She stopped in the middle of the indistinct pathway, shaking her head. He heard her say, "Oh, my God."

She did not move. He walked up close beside her and saw what had stopped her. A man—a youth, really—was propped up against the trunk of a water oak. His face was rigid and his pale blue eyes stared in death. Both his hands gripped at a bloody wound in his belly in agony. Cold blood crusted his denim shirt and discolored his clutching fingers. Flies blackened his hands, the wound, and the corners of his bloody mouth.

Nelle shook her head, ill. "It's Albert Meffert," she whispered. "Poor little bastard. They kept him moving, even when he was dyin'. This was as far as he could make it."

Chapter 16

Longarm sat in the black swamp night with his back against the rough, damp bole of a water oak. He had no idea what time it was. The dark itself was suffocating. He'd felt the blackness closing in like a shroud enveloping them since the first deepening of twilight.

A small fire of damp wood burned fitfully and only intensified the darkness hovering around them. The Thicket thundered with secret noises. Frogs, crickets, mosquitoes, and small, chittering animals raised a timid din. Out in the cypress-black water, alligators grunted, and somewhere a panther screamed.

He watched Nelle Frailey moving around the waning fire and smiled faintly. *What a woman*, he thought.

And what a day it had been. A long, tense accumulation of hours in a wild place where directions were confused, where promising lanes petered into nothingness, and where danger lurked at every step.

Nelle had been equal to any emergency all day. Clearly she knew the forests and ignored the side paths. In her way, she was like the bloodhound with its scent. She was on the trail of one man and nothing could head her away, or deter her, or occupy her mind for more than a few moments at a time. He knew because he had tried.

They had buried Albert Meffert back in the swamp where they'd found him. Digging a grave with a machete and their bare hands wasn't easy, even in the porous mud. The grave they'd scooped out had been shallow and filled with seepage, but they had laid Albert out in it and weighted him down with heavy rocks. The mound over him might protect him from predatory animals.

Nelle had said a quick little prayer for Albert, her head bowed. Then they had strode away along the trail and neither had looked back.

Without Albert to guide them, Blast Haggerty's gang ran into trouble. Longarm and Nelle wasted time following signs that abruptly stopped, broke off, or changed direction totally.

"They won't move very fast now," Nelle said in a savage kind of satisfaction. "Not without Albert to guide them."

They moved warily along the trail. Like a rat finding itself cornered, Blast Haggerty would be more dangerous than ever now that he moved in uncertainty, frustration, and apprehension.

Longarm watched Nelle's pained, taut face relax into sickened contempt. She found places where Haggerty and his men had stopped, paced, and circled, obviously arguing about what direction to take, and likely whether they had been in this place before.

Longarm heard Nelle's savagely chilled laughter once. He said nothing, because he knew the troubled girl did not want to share even her laughter.

"Look at these signs," Nelle said to him, her voice quivering with contempt. "They're totally lost. Here they turned back for no good reason. Here they broke through the underbrush like stampeding cattle. They've given up trying to be smart or trying to hide. All they're trying to do now is find a way out of here. That's the worst thing they could do."

"Look like they're wandering around, all right."

"It's worse than that," Nelle said. "It's panic."

Longarm sat against the tree and watched Nelle prepare for the night. He saw her remove the party dress from her sack and hold it almost tenderly in her slender hands for a few moments before she put it away.

"Don't you want to tell me about it?" Longarm asked.

"Go to hell," Nelle said over her shoulder, without even bothering to glance toward him.

He got up and stretched his mosquito netting from a bayberry bush to the slender sprig of a young elm. Nelle stacked leaves and pine limbs, watching him with interest.

Longarm yawned. Nelle said, "Well, reckon it's time to turn in."

"Great," Longarm said. "Want to crawl in here with me?"

"You keep your place, Long, and we won't have no trouble."

"I'm offering to share my netting with you, Nelle, not anything else. You've said you don't want me. You don't have to keep telling me. I had women before I ever came to this garden spot of East Texas, and I'll have them after I get out of it."

She sighed. "I reckon you've had more'n your share of women—a sprightly-looking devil like you."

"I'm no Blast Haggerty," Longarm teased, "but I do all right."

Longarm got under his mosquito netting. He heard Nelle sigh and sink down upon her pine boughs and leaves. The swamp mosquitoes were huge. Longarm heard them whining around the netting and slamming into it.

He watched Nelle rub the rancid fish oil on her hands, neck, and face. He said, "Once those devils get used to that smell they're going to eat you up."

For a long beat, she said nothing. Then she got up and came across to the netting. He lifted up one side and she crawled in under it.

He moved over, making room for her. Nelle sat for a moment. She drew a hunting knife from its sheath on her belt, gripping it in her palm. "You going to sleep with that thing?" he said.

"No. You are. I warn you, Long, I'll gut you if you touch me."

He laughed. "I think I can remember that."

She lay down beside him on her back, holding the knife on the planes of her flat little belly. "It's nice under here," she said. "I think you're a mighty comely fellow, Long. And if I wasn't so full of hurt, I might be as excited about you as any normal woman—"

"Nobody will ever accuse you of being a normal woman, Nelle," he said. "But you're a lovely young girl. I'm sorry you let Blast Haggerty make you so bitter."

"Forget it," she said. "Go to sleep."

Longarm felt himself responding to the slender girl lying tensely quiet beside him. It didn't make sense—she smelled like decaying fish, and she'd warned him about touching her—but there it was, the growing hardness, the increasing pulse, the warmth around his throat and face.

The night sounds receded around them. They heard the mosquitoes humming in frustration at the netting. Animals and reptiles skittered in the underbrush. The last embers of the fire smoked and winked and paled to ashes.

He heard a gasping sound, as if the girl beside him was unable to breathe. Startled, he opened his eyes and listened.

Nelle was crying. Her body was shaking with sobs that she tried to control, swallowing hard.

"Go ahead," he said. "Let it out, honey. Tell the whole goddamn swamp about it."

She gasped for breath, sobbing. "I got nothing to say."

"You don't want to keep it in you," he said. "It'll only make you sick."

She burst into helpless tears at the kindness in his tone.

He turned toward her. "Tell me about it," he said. "Talk about it, Nelle."

"Go—go to—hell," she sobbed, but she did not move away.

Longarm slipped his arm under her neck, holding her head down on the inner part of his shoulder. She remained taut, but she stayed there, her tears hot against his skin.

Longarm let her cry. He did not know how long they lay there, close, touching, and yet somehow apart. Everything Nelle did she did with all her heart and soul, even her heart-broken weeping.

He smoothed her long dark hair with his hands. He pressed his lips against her fevered forehead in a comforting way that she could not and did not mistake.

After a long time, she pressed closer, sniffling. Her hand closed on his arm, her nails digging into him.

He did not know afterwards how it happened, but she moved so that her shapely young body was outlined against his. She did not retreat from the swollen ridigity at his crotch. He heard

140

her gasp as her crying abated and then she tilted her uppermost leg and settled upon his hardness.

Sighing, he held her close like that for a long time. Now he kissed her tear-salted eyes and the delicate line of her nose. She lifted her lips slightly and he covered them with his mouth. A shudder raced through her.

His hand slipped down the small of her back and touched something on the ground on the other side of her pliant young body. It was her hunting knife.

He smiled faintly and pressed his lips harder, forcing her to open her mouth to his. She quivered visibly and clung to him.

He took his time, but now he was the guide, certain of himself, and confident that he knew the terrain as well as Nelle knew the Big Thicket.

He pressed his tongue between her teeth. She writhed against him, sucking at his tongue and opening her mouth wider to receive it.

His hand loosened the buttons of her shirt, letting her full young breasts spill free. He caressed them for a long time, the nipples growing hard and round, the flesh tightening.

He reached down and loosened his belt and pants. Then he drew her hand down upon his staff. She clutched it in her fingers, and he heard her long, whispered sigh.

"Oh, my God," she whispered.

"What's the matter?"

"Me . . . I'm no damned good . . . I'm nothing but a slut . . . A swamp slut, just like Blast called me."

"You're a sweet and loving little girl."

"No . . . A few minutes ago my heart was broken over the way Blast hurt me. And now, already, I'm grabbing at you like—like a slut."

"Do you want to stop?" he whispered against her face.

She gave a helpless little cry. "Oh, my God, yes. I want to more than almost anything. But I know I can't . . . You're too big, too hard, too hot . . . I can't let go. I've got to have it."

"You'll have it," he whispered. "I promise you, you'll have it."

"Yes . . . But that's what's so insane . . . what's wrong with me? I look at a man and I can't lie down and spread my legs fast enough."

"There's nothing wrong with wanting a man," he said. He unbuttoned her Levi's and slipped them down over her hips. She pushed one leg free and left the pants hanging around one ankle.

He slid his fingers into the heated wetness at her thighs. It was as if she were scalding hot; even her flesh was fevered. He fondled her, worked her, loved her until she was writhing in sweet agony under his hands and pulling at his rod.

She spread her legs and he moved between them. She thrust her hips upward to him and clasped her arms about him. She cried out in a mindless spate of words, meaningless, incomprehensible sounds that seemed torn out of her.

She smashed her mouth against his, taking his tongue as deeply as he could drive it into her throat. Longarm felt himself building up, driven by her heat and madness and frantic appetites. He worked faster and faster, driving his hips to hers, clasping her round buttocks in his hands and pulling her closer. She responded in madness, digging her fingers into his skin.

He felt her rise to a fever pitch. He was aware she was talking to him, but it was as if the words were lost in a cataract of sound, a torrent in his own temples.

For some moments he did not know what she was saying to him, but it did not matter. Then he realized that she was actually saying something, gasping out the same words over and over.

He drove himself to her, overwhelmed by her heat and passion and need. And then he realized she was saying, "You bastard."

Stunned with shock, Longarm hesitated slightly, trying to hear her, to be sure what she said. He'd had a lot of wild words whispered in his ears in his time, but nothing like this.

She whipped her hips upward in helpless rhythm, enslaved for this moment. "You dirty bastard," she gasped. There was nothing loving in her tone, no sweetness, no tenderness. There was only hatred—whether she hated herself, or whether she hated him, he did not know.

She worked faster, whimpering and sobbing in ecstasy, but the faster she moved, the louder she cried in blazing rage, "You bastard."

This strange endearment troubled Longarm. He had never met a woman—certainly not a lovely young girl like this— who cursed him as she devoured him with her mouth and her body.

Driving himself to her, Longarm exhaled heavily. Well, at least it was different. Her wail rose as she trembled in a savage orgasm.

She sagged under him, for the moment spent, but she would not release him. He felt her lock her ankles, one of them cushioned in her Levi's, at the small of his back. She was not about to let him go.

He kissed her, at first lightly.

Nelle trembled, quivering weakly and clinging to him, obviously entranced and delighted with him. And yet all he could really recall was the way she had cursed him in her highest moments of ecstasy.

He grinned. No one could deny that this was at least a unique response to his lovemaking. It was unusual. Different.

What was it they said? Difference was variety, and variety was the spice of life.

She writhed under him, signalling that she was rising to a second fever pitch.

He grinned and drove himself to her. Right now, he had no complaints.

Variety was spicing the hell out of his life.

"You bastard," Nelle wailed. "Oh, you dirty bastard."

She gripped him fiercely, writhing upon him and holding him with all her strength. Her body quivered from her head to her toes.

"Oh, sweet Jesus," she whispered, "I just can't stand it any more."

She fell away from him and Longarm lay there, laughing at her. They had caught the mosquito netting, pulled it from its mooring, and almost wrapped themselves in it.

"You'd better let me fix the netting again," he said, "or we'll be eaten alive."

Sighing heavily, Nelle released him. He carefully lifted the netting and stood up, trying to shake it out and secure it again.

He heard Nelle's half-swallowed whisper. "Longarm. Look out."

He heeled around, grabbing at his belt, but both his cross-draw holster and his gun were gone. He lunged to his knee, grabbing for the shotgun propped against the bole of the water oak tree.

A man's savage laughter stopped him. "Jest kindly hol' what you'uns got, friend. Right there." The voice was high-pitched and strained.

He saw four dark forms surrounding them. One of the men flicked up the glass and lit a lantern. The glow flickered yellowly and then intensified, revealing three men and a woman in homespun denim and handwoven palmetto straw bonnets. They looked as if they had climbed up from a nightmare.

The older man grinned and nudged one of the younger men beside him. "Well, well," he said in that high-pitched twang, "will you'uns jest kindly look at what we'uns got heah."

"A Colt .44 is one thing you've got," Nelle said from under the netting. "And it's fixed right on your gut, old man."

Chapter 17

"Now wait a minute, young woman." The oldest man's voice shook with outrage and disbelief. "You sittin' there naked as an airy jay bird, holdin' a man's gun. You think to kill the four of us with one shot?"

Nelle's voice mocked him. "Whether you've ever seen a woman naked before won't help you much, old man. Just as it won't help you that I can't kill all you swamp rats with one shot. All you better think about is that, no matter what happens, I can kill you with four shots."

The aging man retreated a step. "By God, if'n that there don't jest take the rag off'n the bush . . . you threatenin' to kill me."

"I'm not threatening you, I'm telling you. Any of your people make a move, no matter what it is, you're dead, old man. Think about it."

The old man jerked his head around, checking the two men and the young woman with him to be certain they made no untoward moves. He held up his hand as if ordering them to stand frozen. "We're dealing with a crazy woman here," he said. "Comin' in here goin' to kill ole Luke Scroggings and him jus' tryin' to protect what's his. What kind of hellish jezebel are you anyhow, sister?"

"The kind that can shoot straight," Nelle said.

Luke Scroggings retreated another step.

"You'd best listen to her, Scroggings," Longarm advised in a mild tone. "She belongs here in the Thicket, just like you do. And I promise you she can shoot off a mosquito's tit."

"You jes' kindly relax, sister," Scroggings said to Nelle. "We jes' want to ax you some questions, that's all. We'uns be peaceable folks when we ain't riled by wrongs. We mean you no harm."

"If you want to ask questions," Nelle said, "put your squirrel rifles agin that oak tree yonder. Stack 'em up together and stand away from 'em. That way nobody makes a move that might git you kilt, old man."

Luke Scroggings hesitated for a long breath. His face went rigid under its tobacco-stained mustache and scraggly beard. Thoughts chased themselves like playful squirrels through the high limbs of his mind, but all led to one conclusion. Finally he jerked his head. The other three placed their guns against the bole of the oak tree and backed away. After a moment, Luke Scroggings followed suit.

As unobtrusively as possible, Longarm placed himself between the Scroggings family and their weapons. Also he fixed his clothing. He felt the gaze of the young woman with Scroggings fixed on his pants as he buttoned them. Something like hunger glittered in her strange, dark eyes.

"Ain't you never seed a grow'd man before, woman?" Nelle demanded.

"None 'ceptin' my brothers," the girl said in an odd, breathless voice.

"It's all right," Longarm said in a teasing tone. "I don't mind if she looks at me."

"Well I do," Nelle said. The little swamp girl was as intense in her possessiveness as in her lovemaking.

Startled, he saw that Nelle had been able to struggle into her own Levi's and close them without taking her eyes or the snout of Longarm's Colt from old Luke Scroggings' belt buckle. He grinned. One reason was that all three men—including old Luke himself—were mesmerized by her golden nudity, highlighted in planes and shadows in the lantern light. None

146

of them had ever encountered nakedness to compare with Nelle's, and it was unlikely they would again.

"We been wronged. Bad wronged," Luke Scroggings said at last. "Like I say, we're peaceable folks. But we been bad wronged and we aim to right that wrong."

The girl spoke. "These people ain't the right ones anyways, Paw."

"Shut up, Merelda," Luke said. "How you know they ain't part of that same gang?"

"They don't even look like 'em," Esmerelda said. "I gotten a good look at the five of them, and nairy a one of them looked like this man."

"Even with their pants on," Longarm suggested. "Was the boss of these varmints a handsome, slick-dressing character, Esmerelda?"

She nodded, then shrugged. "He might of been, once. He was pretty muddy and wrinkled and miserable when he come onto our place."

"But smooth-talking?" Nelle suggested.

Esmerelda nodded. "He was so gentlemanly and courteous, even whilst robbin' us, you felt like thankin' him, even when you knowed he was cheatin' you."

"That's him," Nelle said. "That's Blast Haggerty."

"You see there!" Old Luke cried out and looked as if he might gamble his life in a leap for his gun. Then he saw that Longarm barred his way and he looked around, confused and enraged. "You see, they do know them men. They are part of the gang."

One of the younger men spoke. "I don't think they're the same gang, Paw. Them men was Texas riders. I know. I've seen 'em up at Beaumont, down in Galveston . . . High-crowned hats. Buscadero gun rigs. Mexican spurs. These people ain't like them."

"How can you tell?" Luke raged. "And them half naked."

Longarm grinned. "I think he means we wouldn't have stopped by the trail for a little private lovemaking if we had robbed you and were running."

"That's right," Esmerelda said. "They'd be a-movin' fast with the rest of them. Anyhow, they wasn't no woman with them when they was to our place."

Longarm asked, "What's your beef with Haggerty and his

147

band? They've made a lot of people in the Big Thicket hate them. What did they do to you?"

Old Luke opened his mouth to answer, but his rage overcame him and he stuttered slightly before the words would come out right. His hands shook and for a moment he stood and stared in hatred at his trembling fingers.

At last, old Luke was able to speak almost coherently. "I'll tell you what they done to us decent, law-abidin', God-fearin' folk. They come ragin' in our place and assaulted us. They took our food and they stole our means of livin', that's what they done."

"They stole our boats," Esmerelda said.

One of her brothers nodded. "We need them boats for any kind of travelin' we do. Lot better than fightin' these here swamps. We use the boats to check our fish and gator traps, to get oysters and mussels and clams."

"We'uns live on the countryside," Old Luke said. "We eat what is in season—oysters, blackberries, mussels, ducks, deer, rattlesnakes, and alligators. But we'uns got to have our boats if we are to catch any of these bountifuls of God. We got troubles enough. They's good-for-nothin' oil slickin' up most all our well water. Now your friends come in and steal our boats."

"We do need them boats," Esmerelda said.

"It takes time to make a fair-usin' dugout," old Scroggings said. "What is we supposed to live on whilst we makes us new dugouts? Why, we come here to these parts in sixty-one, and this here is the first kind of trouble we ever seed that could starve us out like this here."

"You've lived here all that time?" Longarm said, shaking his head.

"That's right. And we'uns lived well. We'uns believe God will take care of us. His ravens will feed us. That's what we believe. And we hate violence. That's why my woman and I come out here from Georgia when they tried to take me away from her and my farm to fight in some war I didn't no way want no part of."

"And you've been hiding out in the Thicket ever since?" Longarm inquired.

Old Luke shrugged. "We come of our choice. I didn't mean to be kilt in some war I never started and had no part in. If we was hidin' out at first, we decided to stay here and raise our chillun when the war was over. We'uns decided not to go back. Out here we could live peaceable, not bothered by strangers—until your friends come and stole our boats. Good God! They might as well have taken our right laigs."

"Five of them?" Longarm said.

Old Luke nodded. "That's right, as God is my witness. Five of them fellows, meaner than the devil hisself. I ain't no way forgot how to count. There was that slick-talkin', riverboat gambler feller that was the boss, and four others. They was welted up with mosquito bites, but they was plumb runnin' over with the curdled milk of human meanness. That's what they done after they hit me and beat my boys around. They taken all our boats."

"They took our boats," Esmerelda said in a flat voice, cold with hatred. "And they headed down the river in them boats during the night."

Longarm and Nelle looked at each other. Neither of them said anything.

Alone, Longarm repaired the mosquito netting again simply because there seemed nothing else to do after Scroggings and his family had evaporated back into the nightmare swamp from which they had materialized.

Nelle sat and watched him set up the netting like a tent. "Well, ol' Blast has slicked us again," she said.

Longarm nodded. "Looks like it. While we go deeper into the Thicket, he heads out of it in boats."

"We might as well head back," Nelle said after a moment. Her voice sounded oddly unhappy.

"I've got to figure out what Blast means to do with the boats," Longarm said.

"That don't seem so tough to figure to me," Nelle said. "They got no guide. They're eaten up by mosquitoes, hungry, and lost. I know what I'd do."

"I know what I'd do, too. I'd try to get the hell out of here while I was still alive," Longarm said. "But they've still got that stolen money. Where the hell are they going with it? They could run to the nearest town with a railroad track, but that wouldn't buy them a damn thing but trouble. All the trains are being watched by the local lawmen and the Texas Rangers. They can't run by rail."

"If they got to Beaumont, they might buy horses."

Longarm chewed this over for a moment. Then he shook his head. "Horseback would get them out of the Thicket, but it would still leave them in East Texas. Plenty of East Texans are hoppin' mad about the way Haggerty's bunch been robbing and killing."

"You mean plenty of people feel like the folks back at Mortonville? Ready to turn 'em in to the law?"

"They'd be hard pushed to find a friend willing to risk a prison sentence to hide them, even if they could find somebody that didn't hate their guts."

"I don't think that will stop Blast," Nelle said.

"Still admire him, do you?" Longarm teased.

"I admire a skunk if he's a smart skunk. And anybody that thinks Blast Haggerty ain't smart is just foolin' himself."

"All right. So he's smart. And he's rich. But he's still been pushed in here until all he wants right now is to get out and save his skin and his loot. Where would he go?" Longarm shook his head, trying to put himself in the fugitive Haggerty's place. "Where would I want most to go?"

Nelle laughed at him without too much humor. "That's easy to answer for you and Blast. In that one way you're both alike."

"Tell me," Longarm said.

"Oh, you can make love a lot better than Blast, because you are built so wonderful and you think about a woman first and what she wants and not yourself and what you want all the time like Blast does. Blast was born selfish and had a relapse. But he wants to get where he could buy plenty of pretty women and good whiskey. In that way, Brother Long, you're not all that different from ol' Blast Haggerty. Either one of you ran anywhere, that's where your runnin' would take you—to women and whiskey."

Longarm laughed but he didn't bother to deny the accusation. Maybe he and Blast were brothers under the skin. Two professionals, good at their jobs, though on opposite sides of the law.

After a pause, he said, "Maybe. But there's something else I'd want first. And if ol' Blast is as smart as you say, he'd be thinking along the same lines."

"Not women and whiskey? You're crazy."

"Maybe. But first I'd want to be safe. I'd want to go to a place where I was safe and could slow down long enough to catch my breath and breathe easy—*then* the whiskey and women, and not necessarily in that order."

"I don't know any place in Texas where Blast would be safe," Nelle said. "Not now."

"If there was some way he could get out of Texas," Longarm mused.

"Like maybe by boat?"

"Not in the little dugouts he stole from Scroggings, but the gulf-going steamers."

"He'd have to go to Galveston."

"Right. With his money, he could hide out there long enough to find an outgoing ship." Longarm nodded. "Come on, Nelle, we're heading back."

Nelle did not move. She remained where she was under the mosquito netting. She had not yet buttoned her denim shirt over her bare, high-standing young breasts. She gazed up at him narrowly.

"What's the matter?" Longarm said. "Aren't you anxious to get back home?"

"No. I'm not anxious to get back to Mortonville. I've been there, remember?"

"Still, it is home."

"It was."

"It's better than fighting the swamps and mosquitoes."

She drew a deep breath and exhaled it slowly. She glanced up at the dark night sky through the overhanging trees. "Do we have to leave right now?"

He shrugged. "It's too late to try to get any sleep."

"But it's still too early to start."

Longarm peered at her in the darkness and grinned. He joined her under the netting. "You may be right," he said. "Where were we when we were interrupted?"

She put her legs apart, smiling brazenly. "You were just about here," she said.

"Damned if I wasn't."

In fluid movements, she opened his pants and, without wasting a move, she slipped her skin-tight Levi's down over her hips and legs, leaving them hanging on one ankle.

He lay down beside her, caressing her. His mind tried to race ahead to Mortonville, to the river, to the run to Galveston, but she was too lovely, too heated, too exciting. He gave it up

151

and decided to chew on this apple for the moment.

He knelt over her and suckled her breasts. She cried out in delight. "Oh my God," she said, "every time you do that, it aches—down there."

He sucked harder and he felt her hips writhe involuntarily. She stood it for as long as she could and then she swung her leg over him, mounting him as he lay prone. She came down upon him easily, carefully, fully, driving herself upon him.

"Oh Lord," he whispered. "There goes the mosquito netting again."

"Who cares?" she panted.

She dug her nails into his shoulders, bent over him, her hair like a curtain closing out the world, her wide-open eyes fixed on his face. She moved faster and faster until she was driven past reason. Suddenly she whispered it, and then said it aloud in anguished rage. "You bastard . . . oh you bastard . . . you dirty bastard."

Startled, Longarm stared up at her. She was going wild: she certainly loved it with all her mind and body and soul; but curses spilled out of her instead of endearing words.

Ah, well, he thought. Even when he clamped his mouth over hers, Nelle kept repeating it over and over, passionately, wildly, ragingly.

At last she slumped heavily upon him like a sleepy child.

He yawned in exhaustion and held her gently upon him. Nelle seemed to plunge into deep and instant sleep. He caressed her hair, ran his hands along the smooth curves and planes of her back and hips.

He did not know how long she slept. He slipped into a drowsy kind of half-wakefulness, remembering her passionate lovemaking, the way she swore at him, and thinking in spite of himself of Blast Haggerty's gang going down the river in boats toward freedom.

She awoke, clinging to him, their bodies adhering in the hot dawn. She yawned and kissed him, delighted. "My God," she said, "you are wonderful. Have you any idea how wonderful you are?"

"Oh, I'm a real bastard, all right," he said.

She winced, and something stirred deep in her dark eyes, but she said nothing. She pulled away from him reluctantly and began to dress. She got her knapsack and brought out the party dress. "You asked me about this," she said.

"A pretty dress." Longarm watched her.

"Yeah. It cost me. More'n I had, really. I got it so's I could look real pretty for Blast Haggerty. Damn him. He lied and told me it was beautiful and that he liked it."

"I doubt that was a lie."

"He never told nothing but lies." Nelle shivered. "Anyway, you asked me why I carried this dress. I carried it to remind me." She nodded. "It reminds me." She wadded it up in her fist and threw it from her with vehement strength.

Chapter 18

The shallow-draft paddle-wheeler whistled, panted, and squealed its lumbering way into the wharf at Galveston. Beyond the mounds of coal piled high to service the ocean-going steamers loomed the warehouses and freight offices, shutting off the view of the town.

Longarm stood with Nelle Frailey at the railing and waited for the gangplank to be lowered. This was done as soon as an off-ramp had been set in place to accommodate the seasick cattle which had fouled up the entire penned-off stern of the intercoastal craft.

Longarm felt the prickling of anxiety. Instinct told him he was on the right track, hounding the tails of Haggerty and company. But how far behind was he? Could they have crept in here and bought passage out while he chased them down the river from the Big Thicket?

Beside him, he felt Nelle shiver. Part of her anxiety, he knew, was stirred by her arrival in this strange and alien place. But how much of her nervousness stemmed from the fact that she was close behind her faithless lover, Blast Haggerty?

He glanced at her, faintly troubled. He'd wanted to leave her back at Mortonville. She had raged at him. She meant to travel to Galveston, with him or without him; he might as well accept her company. Finally, because it was easier than arguing with her, he gave in. But he still didn't feel right about it. He couldn't escape the thought that as long as Nelle Frailey was beside him, there was a small but fierce barrier between him and Haggerty.

She looked pretty enough, and guiltless enough, even above suspicion in her simple print gingham dress and old-fashioned sunbonnet. But he knew her better. Under that gentle-appearing exterior there was a complex, even dangerous, young woman. She knew how to get what she wanted. And if she wanted Blast Haggerty passionately enough, how far could he trust her?

She had given him no reason to mistrust her to this moment, but they hadn't come upon Blast Haggerty yet. They had not reached a place where she had to choose, or prove her stubborn loyalty.

No matter what, he would watch her carefully, tell her as little as possible, and try to keep her well out of harm's way. He didn't want to have her having to choose between him and Blast Haggerty's wealth with guns drawn.

He forced a smile and gestured toward the mounds of coal. "Well, there's Galveston," he teased. "How do you like it so far?"

"I've liked it so far," she said in a strange, quiet tone.

"Have you?" He grinned. "The smell of penned cattle. A crowded riverboat. What have you found to like so far?"

"I've liked being with you," she said.

A black man driving an open and dilapidated carriage hailed them as Longarm and Nelle left the boat. "Where to, Cap'n?" the black man said. "Where can I take you folks? I knows old Galveston island better than the sand fleas. You tells me where you wishes to go, and I takes you straight there. And it costs you two bits each."

"Fair enough," Longarm said. He touched Nelle's arm to help her into the ancient vehicle.

"You folks got any luggage?" the black man said.

"Just this." Longarm showed him the seed-sack lining in which Nelle had crammed her worldly goods.

The black man nodded. "You folks from up the river, ain't you?" he said. Then he smiled again. "Where I takes you folks?"

"How about a nice boarding house? You know a good one where they might take this young lady?"

"Ain't stayin' there 'less'n you do," Nelle said tensely under her breath.

"Know just the place for both of you," the driver said. "You jes' kindly sit back and enjoy the sights whilst I drive you to the Widder Francis's place."

Longarm walked around the bedroom opening the windows to the breeze in from the Gulf, watching the curtains fill and belly out.

At last he turned and faced Nelle, who sat on the side of the iron four-poster bed, watching him. "You ought to be comfortable here," he said.

"Didn't come to Galveston to be comfortable," she replied.

"Why did you come?"

"Same reason you did, I guess. You might as well know, Longarm, I'm looking for Blast Haggerty too."

"I hope you won't get in my way," he said.

"Why would I do that?"

"I don't know. All I know is that this is a Federal matter. I've got to handle it—if I can—and I don't need you getting in the way."

"I won't get in your way."

He drew a deep breath, hating himself for saying it, but knowing it had to be said. "Don't. And there's no sense in trying to get word to him that I'm after him. I don't want to do this, Nelle, but I'll lock you up in the Galveston jail until this is over if I have to."

She didn't move. Her dark face and black eyes revealed nothing. She just sat rigid and stared at him.

Still troubled with the sense of wrong gnawing at the nerves in the pit of his belly, Longarm walked downtown to the sheriff's office.

A young deputy in the outer office took Longarm's name in to Sheriff Sid Walburn's private office and closed the door. After a moment he returned, smiling.

"Sheriff Walburn says for you to come right on in, Marshal Long." He grinned again. "You'll have to forgive me for acting kind of sour at first. You sure hell don't look like no Deputy U.S. Marshal I ever saw before."

157

When he entered Sheriff Walburn's office he saw that the sheriff and the man in a leather chair beside the sheriff's desk were less than impressed with his appearance. Longarm grinned as he shook hands with the sheriff and his guest. "I know I look pretty shabby. I've been up in the Big Thicket."

Sheriff Sid Walburn laughed. "You hardly needed to tell me, Long. I recognize the mud."

Sheriff Walburn was a well-built man in his forties, his hair touched with gray, his sun-weathered face lined. He wore a gray shirt, open at the collar, with his badge displayed on his breast pocket, lightweight trousers, and high-heeled Texas boots.

"You look like you been in a losing battle with them upriver mosquitoes, Long," the other man said.

"You don't have any other kind of battles with those man-killers, Captain Culver," Longarm said.

Texas Ranger Captain Brant Culver grinned. "That's why I'm proud to be a captain. Trouble up in the Thicket, I can always assign some underling up there."

Longarm had met Brant Culver before. He'd worked with the Ranger captain and knew him to be a dedicated, dependable man, good with a gun.

Brant Culver was somewhere in his thirties, Indian-dark and coyote-thin. His Texas twang was softened to an almost apologetic monotone. He seldom yelled or spoke loudly, yet people listened to him.

A brief taut silence touched them, then the three of them spoke at once.

Longarm said, "You fellows got any word—"

Sheriff Walburn asked, "Find any sign—?"

And, at the same instant, Brant Culver inquired, "You bring Haggerty back alive, Long?"

Longarm laughed. "All that adds up to one thing. We're all three nowhere. No better off than we were when I arrived here in Galveston."

"Well, we might be," Brant Culver said in his soft voice. "Sheriff Walburn has word that Haggerty and the four remaining members of his gang are here in Galveston."

"I hear they are," the sheriff said. "I've not seen any sign of them. But the word persists that they are here."

"They left the Thicket in dugouts," Longarm said. "I know that from witnesses. I found the dugouts and I think they caught

158

one of the flatbottom riverboats down to where they could board an intercoastal paddle-wheeler."

Sid Walburn spread his hands. "I got my paid informants around the county. I don't know whether you approve of that kind of law practice, but I'd be dead down here without paid spies. This time nothing has paid off. No one has brought me any word on Haggerty or his men."

"Still, we're almost dead certain they're here," Captain Culver said. "The Rangers are so sure that they've sent in six men to back me up. I've got them all out nosing around."

"What beats me is why they would come in here, where they know we're watching for them," Walburn said.

"I think they're desperate," Longarm said. "I trailed them around the Thicket for a while. Nothing went right for them up there. They could hide out, but they could also wind up lost, dead, or alligator food. Once that sank in, Haggerty did what he had to do. He gave up trying to hide in the Thicket and took his chance on a getaway."

"How the hell does he expect to get away through my town?" Walburn said.

Longarm grinned tautly. "Has it ever occurred to you, Sheriff, that paying informants can work two ways? You pay for information. You got county money. You can afford it. But Haggerty is rich. His life is at stake. He can meet your payoff prices and beat them. Maybe that's why you've got no word."

"Sons of bitches," Walburn said. "I find any one of them bastards has crossed me, I'll throw his ass in jail."

"But, meantime, maybe Haggerty can buy the time he needs. Maybe he has already bought it," Longarm said.

"What the hell does that mean?"

"I've given it a lot of thought. I think Haggerty is smart enough to know that Texas and most of the western states are closed to him right now. Maybe he's trying to get passage for five on a boat bound for New York."

"New York?" Captain Culver leaned forward.

"Why not? It's a big town. A good place for a man like Blast Haggerty to hole in."

"Makes sense," Culver agreed.

"Don't make no damn sense in this world to me," Walburn said. "What would a man like Haggerty do in New York?"

"Spend his money," Longarm said.

"Who'd expect to find a bank robber from Dodge City

hanging out along Broadway in New York City?" Culver inquired.

Walburn stood up, sweating. He leaned on his fists upon his desk top and stared at the U.S. marshal and the Texas Ranger. "Is there any way we can stop 'em?"

"We can," Culver said, "if they haven't already beat us to the draw. If they've found a boat out already, we've lost them."

Walburn shook his head. "One thing is sure as hell in Haggerty's favor, all right. There are a lot of boats leaving this port every day and every night. They go out with the tides."

"What about shipping schedules?" Culver asked.

"Ocean steamers all leave on a regular schedule," Walburn said.

"Right." Culver nodded. "I'll put men on every outgoing ship. That should make intercepting Haggerty's bunch a little easier."

Longarm shook his head. "I think a steamer, with its printed schedule, would be all wrong for our boy Haggerty. He's too devious for that. He knows the trains are being watched. He figures the steamers are too."

"That leaves them damn tramp steamers," Walburn said. "They sail when they get a cargo."

"That would be my guess," Longarm agreed. "Haggerty would make a deal with one of the tramp steamer captains. Nobody else in on it. They board at the last minute."

"We'll stake out the docks," Culver said. "It's just a matter of plain stubborn pride with me. I won't have Haggerty coming down here in my territory and makin' me look like a fool."

"You'll need a lot of men," Longarm said.

"I've got six. Walburn has six. We'll pull them off everything else."

"We can deputize if we have to," Walburn said.

"I'd be careful about deputizing," Longarm said. "My old grandmother always used to say you get a dozen hounds together and there's sure to be one son of a bitch among them."

Walburn shook his head. "All right. We'll stake out the docks. We'll watch the tramps. We'll scour this town looking for them."

Longarm nodded. "I'll talk around the bars. Sailors, whores—see what I can pick up. If I get any word at all, I'll let you fellows know."

Culver nodded. "We'll give you all the help we can, Long."

"So will we," said Sheriff Sid Walburn.

Longarm shook hands with them and thanked them for their cooperation. Then he grinned, shaking his head. "All us law-men working together," he said. "I wonder why it still looks so bad for our side?"

Brant Culver tried to smile. "Maybe it's just something you et," he said.

Longarm swore inwardly. It was nothing he had eaten that gave him a bleak and pessimistic outlook in the Haggerty business; it was looking facts straight in the eye. The fact was that Haggerty was a smart hombre—maybe too smart for Longarm, the sheriff, and the Texas Rangers.

Five long and patient hours and a dozen half-consumed mugs of beer in every seafront dive and Mexican adobe canteen in downtown Galveston bought him nothing but a pressing kidney problem and a dull headache.

He found relief for his kidneys, but the headache persisted, along with the nagging sense that he couldn't think like Blast Haggerty because Blast had a better mind: sharper, keener and cleverer. Haggerty was out-thinking him at every turn.

Deciding to walk off the throbbing pain in his temples, to clear away the cobwebs and sweat out the effects of the beer, Longarm forced himself to put Blast Haggerty out of his mind for the moment.

He walked in the afternoon sun toward Capo's clapboard shack near the beach. He felt the beer boiling and churning inside him, heated by the sun and soured by the humidity.

He paused a short distance from the tar-paper-roofed hut that crouched as if trying to hide in a whiskered clump of sea oats bearding the sand dunes above the waterline. He remembered Capo and the way the guide had died, the things Capo had said.

"A hell of a way to die . . . but I reckon they ain't no good way . . . Tell Leona not to wait."

Longarm had little to say to Leona, nothing that would help her very much, but he owed her, and he believed she would want to know.

He saw her slumped on the front slab steps of the shack in the sea oats. She wore a cotton blouse and a bright print skirt. She was barefoot and she sat with her legs apart, her knee supporting her right arm and her chin cupped in one hand. She looked as if she'd been sitting this way for a long time. She looked as though she waited for someone, even when she no longer believed he would ever come home to her again.

Longarm stopped before her and removed his hat, the sun braising the top of his head. He tried to smile. "Do you remember me, Leona?"

The black Latin eyes gazed up at him, bleak and without interest. "I recall you. You came one day and hired Capo to guide you into the Thicket."

"Yes." Longarm grimaced. "Well, that's why I'm here."

"You have come to tell me Capo is dead."

He caught his breath. "How did you know?"

She shrugged, looking as if she might sob, as if she would never cry again, as if she had already cried all the tears inside her. "I know. A woman knows these things. If she loves. If she truly loves. She knows...I awake in the night...and I know."

"He spoke of you as he died, Leona. I thought you would want to know."

"I would want to know that Capo loved me?" Tears did blur her eyes now. "I know. As deep as he loved me—I loved him more."

"I'm sorry."

She shrugged again. "The world she will not stop because two nobodies like Capo and me no longer live. I heard that Capo was shot by a swamp man and his body fed to the alligators, so there will never be any trace of Capo on this earth again."

Longarm stared at the beautiful young Mexican woman. "How did you hear this? Who told you these things?"

She spread her hands. "A woman hears many things when she is in my...trade. A man came home with me. He had only a one-hundred-dollar bill to pay me. He said he had no bill smaller and that I should keep it to remember him. But I would never forget him, even if his face was so swollen from mosquito bites that he looked like a gourd or an alligator pear. He told me he would not see me again because he was sailing from the docks tonight on the tramp steamer, the *Cloudgate*— on the midnight tide."

Chapter 19

The *Cloudgate* lay at anchor, tied up alongside the wharf in Galveston harbor. She looked aged, rust-scabbed, and neglected even in the fading twilight.

"She looks like she ain't planning to go nowhere in this world," Captain Culver whispered to Longarm as they stood in concealment.

Longarm nodded. "Still, that might be just what they want to look like," he said. "Anyhow, I think it's worth it to wait."

"Oh, we'll wait," Culver said.

From where they stood in the deepest shadows of a shed overhand, Longarm and the Texas Ranger captain had an unobstructed view of the *Cloudgate*'s gangplank and its portside superstructure. Only nothing was happening up there.

As darkness settled in, the first lanterns were lit aboard the tramp steamer, and a meager few they were. A couple of portholes glowed a wan yellow; one light showed in the wheelhouse and another near the bow. The entire remainder of the ship lay in gathering blackness.

"It don't look promising," Culver said.

Longarm sighed. "If it looked promising, Captain, I'd lay

you odds it would be the kind of gamble that Blast Haggerty wouldn't touch with a ten-foot pole."

"You admire that polecat's brain, don't you, Longarm?"

"He's smart enough to steal a fortune, and he may be smart enough to walk away with it right under our noses. You're damned right I admire his thinking processes. The bastard has been out-thinking us at every turn."

"How do you know he didn't set this up? How do you know he doesn't have us staked out here while he slips away from another pier, or rows out to some boat anchored in the harbor?"

"All I know is, I trust my source. And I don't think even our man Haggerty is smart enough to know I'd stop cattin' through the bars in the middle of the afternoon and go down to the beach to visit my dead guide's grieving woman."

"Still, the man did tell Leona how her man was killed in the Thicket—even how his body was disposed of."

"That was common talk up there. There ain't a lot to talk about in the Thicket. Probably the backwoods people figured Haggerty's men had killed my guide. So when Haggerty heard the truth about that moron Cloyd Lindsey feedin' Capo's body to his pet alligators, he saw that word got around."

They fell silent, watching the dimly lit steamer gentled at dockside. They found no hint of movement on the deck of the tramp. The shadows deepened, but they were motionless pits of darkness, and vacated.

Even in the intense silence of the night wharf no sounds carried from the ship's galley or below decks. The loudest sound on this loading pier was the buoy bells and ships' remote horns as the fog rolled in.

"Jesus, it's quiet," Culver said.

"Yep. Too quiet."

Culver nodded. "You're right. This kind of quiet sure as hell ain't natural."

As the night socked in tight along the waterfront and the town above it grew quiet, Longarm and Culver could hear Walburn's deputies and the six Texas Rangers moving into place in the darkened anchorage.

Longarm cursed inwardly and heard Culver's disgusted swearing under his breath. "Thought we warned them bastards to move quiet," Culver complained. "Jesus, way they're clumping around they'll scare the nestin' birds off Matamoros."

Longarm said nothing. After what seemed an inexcusably

protracted time of fumbling and stumbling in the darkness, the twelve lawmen finally settled.

"Well, they're in place at last," Brant Culver said in dusgust.

Longarm grinned. "Folks in Houston know we're all in place. But maybe the pirates aboard the *Cloudgate* are deaf."

"I still wish we could have gotten warrants and searched that boat. There's a damned good chance Haggerty and his men were smuggled aboard."

Longarm nodded. "You're right. There's a better than even chance that Haggerty is already hiding aboard ship. Maybe his whole crew is. But it's a gamble we couldn't afford, Captain. If we searched that ship and turned up nothing, we also alerted Haggerty—and we lost him."

Culver stirred uncomfortably. "I'm not letting that bastard Haggerty get away. When that gangplank starts up, I'm boarding her."

"Fair enough," Longarm said, though he could see nothing for it except walking seven Texas Rangers into a seagoing ambush. "I'm gambling we don't have to."

He glanced around in the darkness, seeing none of the lawmen and hoping he wouldn't. The deputies had been stationed just inside the lines of workshops, warehouses, and loading sheds. The open piers and the high piles of coal were left unmanned. Longarm's plan was to allow Haggerty's men to cross the pier and reach the gangplank, there to be stopped. They would be denied passage aboard the *Cloudgate* and they would be corraled by armed men moving in from behind them.

He'd set up his barriers. Now they would see if Haggerty knocked them over or went around them.

The silence deepened along with the darkness. The distant sounds of the town waned and died along with the lights in remote windows. Aboard the *Cloudgate* nothing stirred. The steamer looked as if it would be in port forever.

Somewhere in the darkness a deputy tried to muffle a cough, the sound rolling along the dark piers.

Time plodded slowly, clouding along on the chilled, gathering fog. Wind-riffled waves slapped at the dock pilings as the tide came in. If the *Cloudgate* planned to ship out, it would move on the tide. Longarm slumped against the rough wood of the shed. The crest of the tide; that fixed the limit of their waiting.

Mosquitoes wheeled and skidded about their faces, but all

the lawmen had been warned against slapping a mosquito. They suffered in silence.

The wind came in from the southeast, damp and chilled. Longarm grew cramped simply from standing rigid for so long, but he knew better than to move. Shadows shifting even within shadows could be detected down here almost as clearly as sounds.

From the roadway came the sound of men's voices.

Longarm went tense, feeling Culver come to attention in the darkness beside him.

The arrivals were certainly not being stealthy or even quiet. Some sang drunkenly, others swore and argued loudly. They came across the planking making no attempt to be quiet, talking loudly, like carousing sailors returning from liberty in town.

The men approached, staggering, unsteady on their feet, fighting, laughing, talking. They passed between two mounds of coal, heading for the gangplank of the *Cloudgate*.

"Now," Longarm whispered to Culver. "Let's head 'em off at the ramp. I order them to stop. You light the lantern and hold it up high."

Culver breathed out, a sound of assent, but said nothing. Drawing his gun and holding it ready, Longarm walked out and stood in front of the gangplank with Brant Culver in the darkness at his right.

"Evenin', gents," Longarm said. "Why don't you just hold what you got right there?"

On cue, Culver fired a match, lit the lantern, and held it aloft, spraying the men with light and for a second blinding them.

The men forgot to stagger, forgot to yell drunkenly. They lunged away on each side, drawing their guns. They were firing as they retreated.

Bullets sang lethally around Longarm's head. He threw himself hard to the left, getting as far from the reach of the lantern light as he could.

Culver had already set the lantern on the planking and leaped away in the darkness. Somebody fired. A bullet shattered the lantern glass, struck the wick, and the lamp exploded, fire bouncing out in all directions like fiery red marbles.

Longarm heard men running on the deck of the *Cloudgate*. At the same time he heard the deputies and Rangers closing in behind the gunmen. He didn't want to be a target for some-body above on the ship's deck, so he broke and ran for cover.

He glimpsed a dark figure crouched and running up the side of a coal mound. Longarm fired once. The man leaped forward, landing on his belly in the shifting coals.

A burst of crimson flared from up on that mound. A bullet embedded itself into the upright inches from Longarm's face. Longarm dropped almost to his knees and sidled into deeper shadows as the gunman fired again. Crouching in behind a hogshead vat, Longarm gazed up at the mound. For a moment he saw nothing, then he caught the movement of a man clam-bering upward in downsliding clumps of coal near the crest.

He pressed against the damp barrel, leveled his gun on the shifting coal and the man fighting his way through it. He fired. For one moment, the scrambling figure kept climbing against the avalanche of disturbed coal. Then, as Longarm raised his gun to fire again, the fellow lost his balance, staggered, fell backward, and came thundering down the coal mound in a torrent of black rocks.

One down, Longarm thought, *and four to go.*

They were firing wildly in the darkness. Longarm hugged against the barrel, looking for a target and cursing because in that confused gunplay he couldn't tell friend from foe. This threatened a senseless slaughter.

He heard the whisper of sound behind him. He jerked his head around, bringing his gun into place in the same motion. Someone leaped up from the deep shadows and ran. Longarm couldn't see how in hell one of Haggerty's men had been able to get in back of him, and yet it didn't make sense that a lawman would be running away when all he had to do if he was scared was to hole in until the shooting stopped. So Long-arm fired once, just for the hell of it.

The dark running figure yelled, whether in pain or panic Longarm couldn't tell. Then he fell or jumped over the edge of the pier into the water between the anchored ship and the wharves. Longarm heard the splash of water and then there was silence from down there.

Around him, beyond the high piled coal, guns blazed, a discordant madness. From the town people yelled, running and racing toward the harbor.

It was as if this slice of time were removed from the steady progression of hours. The firing must have lasted only seconds, yet it seemed an eternity of noise and flashing guns. Men cursed, yelled, and sobbed in mortal agony.

Someone yelled through a bullhorn from the deck of the *Cloudgate:* "What the hell's going on down there?"

Longarm yelled back, "U.S. marshal and Texas Rangers making arrests. Stay out of it and—"

There was the crack of gunfire from the deck and Longarm lunged behind the barrel. Even before he set himself he was firing toward the man with the bullhorn.

On deck, the man shouted in terror and the shots ceased. Longarm waited, but nothing happened from the ship. The gunfiring had moved away from him, between the coal mounds and toward the sheds and the deputy-barred exits.

Longarm got up warily from behind the barrel. In the darkness he reloaded his Colt, then ran along the plankings toward the sounds of the waning gun battle.

As Longarm ran between the mounds of coal, the gunfire abated and lantern light began to show all along the wharf and the road behind it as people funneled into the area.

"Stop those people out there," Longarm yelled toward the street. "Keep them out of here."

The lanterns converged and Longarm slowed, halting in the middle of carnage. Sheriff's deputies were dragging bodies from the darkness and stacking them in a line under the lantern light.

"Four of them," Brant Culver was saying. "We got them, Long."

"How many of our people are hurt?"

"A couple winged. Deputy named Clemonts might be hurt more serious," Culver said. "We got off light."

Longarm walked slowly, staring at the lantern-lit corpses. The mosquito-swollen faces were almost all the identification he needed. These were four of the men who had run into the Thicket and then had come out of it. They were none too handsome, even allowing for the distress they'd suffered in the swamps. They looked like what they were: hardened criminals, Texas riders who had taken up the profession of bank robbery.

Something nagged at him, stopped him, and jarred him like a fist in the jaw. Not one of these men matched the description he'd been given of their leader. Blast Haggerty was not among the corpses.

Culver said it before Longarm could put it into words. "Blast Haggerty—he ain't here."

Longarm stared at the corpses as if willing one of them to take on the form and characteristics of the leader. Hell, he should have known better. Blast Haggerty never walked into anything without leaving himself a way out.

"Son of a bitch." Longarm spoke under his breath. "Haggerty has fooled us again. He let his men walk into the trap and he held back."

"Or else he's already aboard that ship," Culver said. "That's what I'm going to do, and I'm going to do it now. What I wanted to do all along—search that ship. As soon as I get this mess mopped up, my men and I are going to board the *Cloudgate*, and we'll tear her apart inch by inch until we find that rat."

Chapter 20

Longarm wasted no time on the mopping-up operations. He could count, and he had Blast Haggerty's description pretty fully set in his mind, and it took no great perception to see that the man he wanted most, the prize old Billy Vail was after, was not among the bodies stacked like cordwood at the piers.

He heeled around and ran through the island darkness. The Texas Ranger who had been jawing at him stopped talking in mid-sentence and yelled, "Hey, Long! Wait a minute! Where the hell are you going?"

Longarm didn't bother to answer. He pushed his way through the crowds and the lawmen holding lanterns high along the docks. It looked as if most of the town of Galveston had been attracted to the coal yards by the gunfire.

Holding his gun by its butt in its cross-draw holster, he ran out of the yard, pushed his way through the gawking bystanders, and strode along the street toward downtown Galveston.

At the first fringe of business buildings he slowed, checking every side street, alley, and shadowy cranny where a fugitive gunslick might hide.

He knew what he was looking for, but he had no idea where in hell Blast Haggerty could have disappeared to in that hail of gunfire. Only two things seemed certain: Haggerty would have the loot with him; and this escape was part of the outlaw's contingency plan.

Longarm swore under his breath, hurrying through the poorly illumined darkness. He knew Blast Haggerty's mode of operation well enough by now to know that the bandit leader left nothing to chance. The last detail was well chewed over and mapped out in advance. On matters such as life, escape, and loot, there would be no margin left for error. Blast Haggerty was the kind of gambler who never gambled. In the risk-taking profession, he never took risks.

Longarm stepped into a hole, twisted his ankle, and cursed under his breath. He staggered along until he caught his balance. These damned island streets were paved with shell, but their shoulders were all deep-rutted sand.

Longarm slowed. His ankle ached just enough to keep him constantly aware of it every time he set one foot in front of the other. He moved with extreme caution because no matter what goal was in Blast Haggerty's well-laid plans, the gunman couldn't have gotten too far from the docks yet. There were only limited accesses for a man trying to leave Galveston island in a hurry—the ferry, the railroad, and the gulf-going steamers. The Texas Rangers had just about shut off Haggerty's chances of boarding an outbound ship. Still, one option remained open to Haggerty. A man with as much money as Blast Haggerty now held as sole owner could work all sorts of minor and sordid miracles. Every man had his price, and Blast Haggerty could buy most of the denizens of Galveston island with what was to him by now pocket change.

Longarm paused in the middle of the dark and shadowed street. Except for a whisper of sound behind him, unexplained but quickly gone, the whole seaport lay in stunned night silence.

He gazed at the dark houses, the shuttered shops, the loud saloons. The Mexicans drank quietly in adobe cantinas. Indians merely slumped, incurious and disinterested in the white man's strange ways of destroying himself, his enemies, his friends, and his surroundings.

The entire town was quiet, seeming to hold its breath, waiting. The silence was different from that up in the Big Thicket, but it held the same peril, the same threat.

Longarm knew this tension had to be in his own imagination, but it was just the sort of vision that could add to the sweat already staining a man's shirt and burning his eyes in the humid night.

Longarm chewed at his mustache. There were two ways to handle this manhunt, neither of them terribly promising. He could barge ahead until he picked up a sign of some sort as to what Haggerty planned. Not even Blast Haggerty could disappear without a trace from this island, not even in the dark of night. Still, barging ahead was one good way to stumble into ambush and get your head blown off.

He breathed out raggedly. He had to be smarter than that. He had to be smarter than Blast Haggerty if he hoped to stay alive long enough to stop the outlaw.

And that left the second option open to him in hunting down Haggerty. He could try to think like Blast Haggerty, like a harried man, rich as hell, but abruptly alone in an alien world of ordinarily law-abiding citizens. Blast Haggerty had seen the last of his wild bunch chopped down in a hail of bullets. That had to stir panic even inside so cool a customer.

Still, at this moment, Haggerty's life and his ill-gotten fortune were at stake. Blast Haggerty was running like a pursued rat; he would use all the guile and cunning and vicious trickery in his mental arsenal.

Longarm moved forward cautiously, stealthily. His mind kept spitting up the single word: hideout. *Hideout. What would I do if I were suddenly the last of a band of owlhoots, trapped on an island crawling with Texas Ranger guns?*

Hideout.

Nothing else made sense. It was as if everything suddenly became clear in Longarm's mind. A hideout in case the best-laid plans went up in gunsmoke. Hole in somewhere and sweat it out. Right now, Blast Haggerty needed more than anything else a place to burrow in and rest up and lick his wounds, and make his new plans.

Longarm moved out of the street into the shadows at the verandas and overhangs of building fronts. He moved step by step now, testing every doorknob.

He reached out for a door latch and stumbled on something. He might have missed it except for the tenderness in his ankle. He shifted one foot forward and, instead of putting all his weight on it, tried to shuffle ahead.

He paused, looking down. What at first looked like a wadded bandana lay on the dark boardwalk.

Kneeling, Longarm took the damp fabric up in his hand. He recoiled slightly at the wet feel and the sickly-sweet smell of fresh blood. It wasn't a bandana at all. It was a man's large white linen handkerchief, sodden with blood.

His heart pumped faster. Blast Haggerty hadn't walked away from the battle unscathed, after all. Blast Haggerty, bleeding profusely, had passed this way. He couldn't be too far ahead.

Longarm shoved the bloody handkerchief into his hip pocket. He pressed against the wall and sidled along the rough planking, feeling it scraping into the flesh of his shoulder.

Holding his gun, he inched along in the deepest shadows until he reached the corner of an alley. He lifted his foot to step out and off the boardwalk, then changed his mind. Removing his hat and holding it behind him, he peered around the edge of the building.

The alley was narrow, little more than a littered air space between two false-front adobe buildings. A cat spat from the shadows. Nothing else moved down there. He waited, watching the darkness. Then, replacing his hat, he padded across the narrow alley to the next row of buildings.

The first store space was deserted. Cans, newspapers, and other debris sprinkled the walk and the recessed entry.

Longarm side-stepped into the deep shadows of this dark and smelly foyer. With his left hand, he reached out and touched the doorknob.

Shocked, he almost withdrew. He encountered that same sticky, spongy wetness of fresh blood he'd found on the handkerchief. And, more than that, the door stood ajar, perhaps half an inch. Then he saw that the heavy old lock had been smashed and hung warped upon its metal hook.

He touched his finger to the trigger of his Colt, holding it ready at his side. Taking a deep breath as if about to plunge into unknown waters, Longarm set himself on his sore ankle and lifted his foot to kick the door open wide.

The sound behind him was less than a whisper. But in Longarm's mind it was like the roar of savage, taunting laughter. He had been suckered. He had bought the hideout idea, the bloody doorknob, the broken lock.

He tried to heel around in the confining space, but he didn't make it. Something—a hard-swatted gun butt—struck him in the crown of his head.

He pitched forward. His shoulder struck the panel and the

door flew open, batting loudly against the inner wall.

Longarm plunged outward, face-first. He tried to hold on to his Colt, but the big gun was too heavy for his suddenly numb and paralyzed fingers.

The gun clattered to the floor and rattled away, lost in the darkness. Longarm did not really care. He was overwhelmed by the pain radiating downward from his skull.

Pain exploded in the crown of his head and reverberated behind his knees. His legs went as weak as whey. His teeth hurt. His eyes felt as if they'd be driven from their sockets by the terrible inner pressure and jangled, crossed nerve-ends.

He struck the floor without even being able to break his fall. There was the sound of grinding timber, a volley of dust clouding up around him.

It was too quick, too wild for a thought, too isolated in those muddled mental processes inside his brain, but through his mind raced one raging question, unanswered and agonizing. *Why didn't he just kill me on sight and get it over?*

"All in good time, Long," said the smooth, urbane riverboat gambler's voice, as if answering Longarm's question. "I'd have put a bullet in you some time ago when I first noticed you trailing me, but I can't afford to draw a crowd like the one you fellows attracted to that massacre at the coal yard."

Longarm heard Haggerty's taunting voice, but it was distorted, as if from across a great distance. Haggerty's tone grew stronger, faded, and then ran together, a discordant wailing inside Longarm's ears.

Instinctively, Longarm reached out, groping on the dark floor for his gun.

The soft, derisive voice raked at him in the painful darkness. "No use looking for your gun, lawdog. It's out of reach. It's too late now, anyhow. You won't need a gun where you're going."

This idea of a long, one-way voyage for the lawman seemed to delight Haggerty and he toyed with it for an extended beat, savoring the words on his tongue.

"You just wouldn't stop tailing me, would you, lawdog?" Haggerty's polished tone sliced with reproach. "You and those Rangers. You bastards set upon my men as if they were animals. You killed them mercilessly, as you might kill mad dogs. You should have stopped there."

I promised somebody I'd bring him your gizzard, Longarm

answered deep in the pain-riven recesses of his mind. Haggerty didn't hear him, but it didn't matter. Longarm just wished the brain-numbing pain would stop pulsing in his rear teeth for a moment. The agony in his skull was bad, but it was nothing like that ache blasting at the roots of his back teeth.

"A man like you," that modulated, well-bred voice pursued Longarm into the pain-slimed morass where he wallowed, "a man like you *asks* to be killed, lawman. You beg for it. You don't have sense enough to know when to stop." Haggerty laughed faintly. "Or did you think to shake me down? Eh? Was that why you kept following me when ordinary lawdogs would have given up? Well, I regret to inform you, fellow, no payday for you. I've been through hell for this money. Too many people have died making sure I got it and kept it." He laughed mildly. "I owe it to those dead men to live well on every penny of it."

A prolonged silence stretched across the empty room. For this, Longarm was thankful, until it occurred to him that perhaps Blast Haggerty had continued talking but that his sense of hearing had failed him.

He lay, sweating and suffocating in that vile pool of physical torment, aware that his crossed and ragged nerve-ends were gradually quieting. His teeth no longer ached piercingly; the pain ebbed, dull and regular, finally bearable. He could think about something else.

Somehow, lying there, all he could really think was that it was too late for planning, for options, for taking advantage of any last-minute opportunities. It looked as if Custis Long had finally met more than his match in Blast Haggerty and had reached the end of his trail at the ass-end of Texas in somebody's abandoned storeroom.

His right arm hurt, curled up under him. He tried to move and his hand closed on the butt of his derringer. He caught his breath and held it. He marshalled all his powers of concentration and ordered his numbed fingers to move, to grasp, to close. His hand shuddered, struggled. He managed to loosen the clip on the chain. After what seemed an eternity, his fist closed on the gun handle.

He set himself for the gamble. The odds were staggering against his being able to turn onto his back and fire the little double-barreled hideout. If he moved a muscle, Haggerty would start beating his brains out again. If he didn't move, he lost. Plainly, Haggerty meant to pound his head to pulp either way.

He sucked in a deep breath and set himself.

In mid-movement, Longarm canceled all messages from his brain center. Shivering, Longarm became aware that Haggerty was kneeling over him, hovering, as if waiting for the tiniest move. The bandit's voice sounded close, genteel, cultured— deadly. "Sorry we have to do this in such a painful way, old man. I personally have no stomach for violence. But, on the other hand, beating you to death with a gun butt seems to be my only choice. Messy but quiet."

Behind them, a whispered sound shattered the tense stillness, almost like a cat's paws on the floor. Then there was the dry whimpering of rusty hinges and the door was pushed open.

"Blast."

It was a woman's voice.

The tone and quality were familiar to Longarm, but, for the moment, with his senses addled and nerve-ends raw with pain, he could not identify the person who spoke in that soft, reproachful tone from the doorway.

Blast Haggerty recognized the intruder. The breath sobbed out of him as if he'd been kicked suddenly in the crotch.

He lunged around, levering himself up from his knees. A long, breathless pause hung in the room. Then Haggerty managed to speak in that suave, unruffled tone. "Nelle. Thank God you're here."

"Yes." Nelle's voice was flat and forlorn. "Thank God I found you. I was afraid you'd get away from me, even though you promised you'd never leave Texas without me."

"How'd you find me, honey?"

Nelle sighed heavily. "I followed Long here. I figured he'd be looking for you."

"It don't matter. Thank God you're here. That's all I care about now. I need you, Nelle honey. As never before. I got plugged—back there at the docks. I don't think it's fatal, but it's painful as a toothache and it slows me down some. If you can dig out the slug and patch me up, we can get out of here— two rich Texans off to see the world."

Nelle hesitated. "I'm through fixin' you up, Blast. That's all over. When I fix you this time, you'll be just another jewel in Satan's sordid crown. That's the way the minister talks about you, back home."

"That stupid bastard," Haggerty said between clenched teeth.

"Oh, I don't know," Nelle said. "Pastor Dexter was smart enough at least to get something out of you besides a pack of lyin' and sweet-mouthin'...But nothin' you can say will do you any good with me."

"Don't be a fool, Nelle."

"No. I'm through being your fool too, Blast."

Blast tried to laugh, but laughter proved painful too. He coughed. "Aw, come on, honey...You knew I was going to take care of you all along. I was going to send for you." Some of the oiliness in his voice clogged in its own urgency.

"Were you, Blast? Going to send for me, like you promised—"

"You know I was, sweetheart—"

"Where from, Blast? Paris?" Her voice was edged in irony. "Aw, that would've been nice."

"It would've been, Nelle."

"You don't stop lyin' even when you're five seconds from dyin', do you, Blast?"

"Listen to me—"

"No. I got where I am by listening to you. I know now you never meant to take me nowhere except to the nearest haypile when you got a hard-on."

"That ain't true, Nelle. I want to take you with me. Now. Tonight. And I will take you with me, Nelle. I've got all the money now. Every penny. It's all ours. See those two satchels? We can live high, Nelle, just like I told you all along."

"You think I'll listen to your stupid lies any more, Blast? When I believed your lies I was a stupid swamp girl. An easy fuck for a man like you. Anything you wanted. I'd never met or even hoped to meet any man as cultured and handsome and genteel as you, Blast. I never knew there was men like you anywhere."

"And that's the way I felt about you, honey. You were sweet. Unspoiled."

"Stupid, Blast. You can say it. I was stupid."

"No. You were lovely. Untouched. Unspoiled."

"Yeah, I reckon. But now I've been spoiled. By you. But even that don't matter no more, Blast. It hardly hurts at all any more. I've met a better man than you, Blast. A real man. Bigger. Harder. More gentle. Caring. He made me see what a make-believe man you were, Blast, not a real man at all. He made me see how little I had with you."

"You'll forget all that—"

"I won't never forget nothing—"

"I'll make it up to you."

"No, Blast. It's over. I loved you more than anything in this world, and now I hate you more'n I even knew I could hate. It's over for you." And, as if she had coldly pronounced judgment, Nelle as coldly carried out the execution.

Lying sprawled face-down, Longarm could not see what happened. But it was the kind of brief and final violence he didn't need to witness. He saw it etched in his own mind: the trick was to be able to expunge it.

Nelle's gun spoke once from just inside the door. Nelle was a swamp girl, swamp trained. She'd learned to shoot where shooting straight made all the difference between eating or going to bed with a hungry belly. Nelle couldn't miss with a gun. And she didn't.

There was the sharp eruption of gunfire, illumining the bare, musty room for one brilliant instant and then flashing for some seconds behind Longarm's eyeballs.

The bullet struck Blast Haggerty full—and directly and fatally—in the center of his chest. One moment he stood, urbane and smooth-talking, rich and self-assured: the next he sprawled across the floor in the darkness.

Longarm went on lying there for a moment. Nothing happened. There were sounds of shouts and running feet on the shell pavement and the resounding boardwalks but they were all distant, remote, as if the shell-paved street were an avenue on the moon.

Then he became aware that Nelle Frailey was kneeling beside him.

"Are you all right?" she said.

Longarm sighed. "I've been maybe nearer death. But I never hurt worse," he whispered.

"You want I should help you up?"

"Unless you want to lie down here with me."

"I reckon them Texas Rangers will be along soon."

"I reckon."

Her voice scratched at him like urgent cat claws. "There's two satchels of money, Long. We could go a terrible piece from here together."

"Running. If we took that money we'd be running, Nelle. All our lives. Like Blast Haggerty was running. In style, but always looking back over our shoulders."

She exhaled and shook her head. "I reckoned you'd turn me down. Knew inside the kind of lawman you are."

"Reckon we can't go against what we are inside even when we ought to have sense enough to know better."

"No. I reckon we can't. That bastard Blast Haggerty proved that. He was rotten inside, no matter how pretty he looked on the outside . . . the bastard."

He stirred slightly, remembering the way Nelle had cried out those words at the wildest crest of her orgasm. "So Blast is the bastard you keep talking to."

"The dirty bastard."

Longarm laughed, incredulous, even though the laughter made him feel as if the back of his head were flying off. "And all that time at those hottest moments when you were calling me a dirty bastard, you weren't thinking of me at all. You were thinking of ol' Blast."

"No." Nelle shook her head. "I was *thinkin'* about you. And nothin' but you and what a hellish total stud you are, Long. But I was remembering that prize bastard on the floor there. The man who took my cherry. The man who sweet-talked me all the way into hell. The man who made me think what he gave me was the best in the world. Now I know it wasn't even any good. The man I loved more'n anything in this world. Ol' Blast Haggerty."

"I thought—from all you said—that you still loved him and always would. That party dress to remind you—"

"To remind me how much I hated him. How little I had really meant to him, even when I spent my last penny tryin' to look pretty for him. I wanted him to be proud of me, like I was of him. But he didn't even care. Oh, I loved him, all right. My own true love. I loved Blast Haggerty above all men, but what he really taught me was to hate—not to love at all—to hate fiercely and with all my heart."

She sighed, her voice catching in her throat. "I'll miss you, Long. Truly miss you."

"You've got a beautiful life ahead of you, Nelle. One thing ol' Blast Haggerty proved to you, Nelle: you're a beautiful, desirable, lovely woman—"

180

She gulped.

"You just get out of that Thicket and give yourself a chance—"

"It's you I want a chance with," she whispered in a forlorn tone.

"You know better, Nelle. You're what? Eighteen? You want a man who'll come home to your bed every night. I couldn't ever promise you that, Nelle, even if I was young enough for you. I am what I am—a lawman. I lay there inches from death when you walked in. Blast planned a savage, bloody kind of death for me—"

"But I came in—"

"You did this time. But I couldn't put you through that kind of hell, day in and day out. Waitin' at home while I tiptoe along a precipice inches from death, but God knows where. Marriage to me is no life for any woman. It's sure as hell no way for a young girl like you to try to live."

She was silent for several moments. People ran past the vacant store outside, shouting to each other, their boots loud on the boardwalk. Her voice was low, little more than a faint whisper. "You're really sayin' this is your kind of life—the only kind you want—bein' a lawman—"

"It's all I know, Nelle. All I am."

"—and you wouldn't give it up for me."

He smiled and touched her chilled hand. "As soon for you as for any woman, Nelle. It's just I can't go against what I am. I can't lie to you about that."

She sucked in a lonely, sad little breath. "How will I get along without you?"

"A pretty girl like you? In a whole new life? Away from that Thicket? It'll be easy. Easiest thing you ever did. I don't even like to think how easy it will be."

Nelle crouched there, silent, for a long time. "Are you— leaving Galveston—soon?"

He sat up and took her hands, smiling at her in the darkness. "Soon, Nelle. But not that soon."

"You think I'll be used to the idea of you leaving me by the time you have to go?"

"I guarantee it. I promise you'll be so tired and sore you'll be glad to see me go."

Nelle took his hand. Her own chilled hands trembled. But

181

she smiled and nodded. "That sounds good. We'd best get started. Can you walk?"

"To the nearest hotel? Hell, I'll outrun you!"

"No, you won't." She giggled in the darkness. "You'll walk. Nice and slow and easy. Leaning on me. I want you to save your strength."

Watch for

LONGARM AND THE EASTERN DUDES

forty-ninth in the bold
LONGARM series from Jove

coming in November!

LONGARM

Explore the exciting Old West with one of the men who made it wild!